CAMERON
TIBERIUS MCPHERSON
AND HIS MAGIC CHAIR

TUG J. WILSON

CANDY JAR BOOKS · CARDIFF
2021

The right of Tug J. Wilson to be identified as the
Author of the Work has been asserted by him in accordance
with the Copyright, Designs and Patents Act 1988

Cameron Tiberius McPherson and His Magic Chair
© Hoho Entertainment Limited 2021

Hoho Entertainment Contributory Editor: Oliver Ellis
Candy Jar Editorial: Keren Williams, Will Rees

Printed and bound in the UK by
Severn, Bristol Road, Gloucester, GL2 5EU

ISBN: 978-1-913637-70-5

Published by
Candy Jar Books
Mackintosh House
136 Newport Road, Cardiff, CF24 1DJ
www.candyjarbooks.co.uk

All rights reserved.
No part of this publication may be reproduced, stored in a
retrieval system, or transmitted at any time or by any means,
electronic, mechanical, photocopying, recording or otherwise
without the prior permission of the copyright holder. This book is
sold subject to the condition that it shall not by way of trade or
otherwise be circulated without the publisher's prior consent in
any form of binding or cover other than
that in which it is published.

Dedicated to Cameron McMillan and Lucia Santa Maria
— for the good times!

CHAPTER ONE

A TORNADO COMES

'It's summer time on 51.4 FM,' rang out the radio jingle. 'This is Radio Pimple at 9.00 am, where the sun always shines. But today, we are issuing a severe weather warning. A tornado is approaching the city of Pimple at high speed. The council have asked everyone to stay indoors and to secure all windows and exits. Please ensure...' At which point, the radio lost its signal and cut out.

'Ensure what?'

Cameron Tiberius McPherson was an inquisitive nine-year-old boy with a round face and lively brown eyes. His nose and cheeks were covered in freckles and the brown hair on top of his double crown stuck up in the air. He wheeled himself over to the window in his wheelchair and watched as dark smoky-grey clouds rolled in from the distance towards his home on the seventeenth floor of Grimthorpe Towers. The first roll of thunder bellowed out ominously.

'We don't get tornados here, do we, Mum?' Cameron asked Lulu. Lulu was Cameron's devoted mother. She was an eccentric woman with a flamboyant dress sense, a love of rock 'n' roll and a devil-may-care attitude. Cameron's friends always told him that his mum was nuts. Certainly, they shared the same nutty sense of humour, although humour was the farthest thing on Lulu's mind this particular morning.

Lulu dashed over to the telephone and picked it up. The lines were down. 'Blast!' she uttered anxiously under her breath.

From his window, Cameron could usually see the skyline of the town of Pimple as clear as day. But today he thought, rubbing his eyes, it was like looking out through his glasses before he'd cleaned them. He could just make out the smeared shape of the Post Office tower building in the distance. The brand-new shopping mall now looked like a featureless black Lego building. Potwell Park and the private Gitwick Gardens were nothing more than dirty green smudges. The darkened skies had caused the inhabitants of Pimple to switch on their lights earlier than normal but the oncoming storm was causing havoc with the electricity supply and the lights seemed to flicker and sizzle as the electricity came and went.

It was kind of spellbinding. Cameron stared as he saw the swirling tornado twist and turn nearer and nearer.

Lulu quickly flicked the light switch but there was no electricity. 'Candles,' she muttered to herself as she rushed into the kitchen and rummaged in a cupboard.

The tornado roared closer, moving at a terrifying speed in the direction of Grimthorpe Towers. Cameron watched in horror as it tore the tiles off the roofs in its way, scattering them like confetti. The colossal coil scooped up anything and everything in its path.

A slate tile suddenly smashed through the window. The wind howled in, hurling the shattered glass against the wall into the red, quilted exterior of the cocktail cabinet.

'MUM, HELP!' Cameron cried.

Lulu ran from the kitchen into the sitting room.

'Oh my life,' she shrieked, clutching the pearls around her neck.

'Mum, what do we do?'

'Don't move!' said Lulu and she raced back into the kitchen, emerging again with a coiled washing line. She pulled Cameron in his wheelchair over to the corner of the room farthest from the window, sat next to her son on a dining chair and wrapped the washing line around them both, tying them securely together.

'What *are* you doing, Mum?'

'I don't really know,' admitted Lulu, 'but I feel a lot safer now.'

Cameron looked up. The wind was buffeting the ceiling light up and down, this way and that.

SMASH! The 1950s ceramic shade hit the ceiling and shattered above them, scattering broken pieces all around.

'Muuuuumm!'

Although her heart was pounding with terror, Lulu's voice remained calm. 'Don't be frightened, Cameron,' she said. 'We're tied together securely, nothing is going to happen to us.'

At the very top of Grimthorpe Towers perched a weathervane, fashioned in the shape of Zephyr, the god of the west wind. Cameron and Lulu listened to its rusty screech as it was buffeted back and forth by the storm above. Eventually, with a large crack, Zephyr was wrenched from his concrete roots and hurled into the maelstrom. Cameron and Lulu watched in terrified awe as his oxidised face and twisted smile flew past the broken window frame, looking in at them before swirling around and being sucked up into the sky.

Cameron had never experienced anything quite like it. It was the first time he had ever felt a building tremble, its walls shake. He put his fingers in his ears to block out the sound of the banging kitchen and bedroom doors, convinced they would tear off their hinges and fly through the room. Lulu wrapped her arms around him, trying to cover his face. But

Cameron couldn't help watching. It was strangely compelling. The sky flashed bright white, momentarily blinding them both.

'Was that lightning?' he gasped. A split second later, his eyes adjusted. Amidst the drama of the twirling twister, he thought he could see a multi-coloured van driving calmly through the sky, with flashing green and pink headlights. Its psychedelic exterior was a vivid contrast to the black and grey hues of the tornado. Cameron thought he could just make out a shadowy shape behind the wheel.

'Mum, Mum, look! I think... that's an ice cream van driving through the sky.'

'For goodness' sake, Cameron,' said Lulu, holding him close.

'Honestly, Mum, it's true, it's true!'

'OK, OK, Cameron, I'm sure you're right,' Lulu soothed, determined to comfort her son. Elvis was the answer. She knew every Elvis song off by heart, inside out and back to front. She had always found comfort in the King's songs. Now was the time for Elvis.

'Love Me Tender, Love Me True...'

The sound coming from his mother's throat never ceased to amaze Cameron. Lulu was never the best of singers. But as her singing continued, the oddest thing happened – the storm started to calm down.

Mum's singing is SO bad, it even scares bad weather away, Cameron thought to himself.

It was true: the twister rapidly dropped away and the wind that had caused so much havoc disappeared as quickly as it had arisen. As Lulu croaked through the last verse, glimpses of blue sky emerged amidst the grey clouds.

'Well at least you're smiling again,' said Lulu as she untied the washing line, got up from her chair and walked tentatively into the middle of the room to assess the damage. She raised her hand in the air to halt Cameron from following her. 'Stop, Cameron! There's glass everywhere.' She rushed into the kitchen to grab a broom.

The two of them spent the next two hours attempting to put the room back together again. So many of their cherished objects were broken or damaged and there was so much to do that they both went about the clean-up operation silently glum.

Cameron bent down from his wheelchair and carefully picked up the pieces of the previously wall-mounted reproduction of Elvis Presley's guitar. The fretboard was broken in two with rough splinters at the shattered edges. Lulu placed her beloved Hawaiian lamp, with its straw shade and the now cracked china Hula girl, back onto the retro sideboard. She was finding it difficult to keep back her tears. A lifetime's collection of beautiful and unusual objects broken or destroyed within the space of an hour.

'Well at least there's some good news, Mum. Your Elvis Presley memorial plate is still in one piece.'

'Thank heaven for small mercies!' said Lulu.

Cameron gingerly approached the broken window. Looking down at the catastrophe that the tornado had left, his heart sunk. He could hear the sounds of police and ambulance sirens, punctuated by howling dogs. Buses had been overturned, cars were floating in the lake in Potwell Park and trees had been snapped in half as easily as matchsticks. The roof of the local church had been stripped of its tiles and the local market stalls had all blown away, their stripy awnings hanging from rooftops and dangling from trees.

'It doesn't look like Pimple anymore,' said a crestfallen Cameron. Lulu stood behind his chair, gently massaging his shoulders. They both stared for a long time at the broken town in front of them.

Lulu picked up the phone, but the line was still dead. She turned on the television. That didn't work either. There was no radio, no electricity and no gas.

'Oh my days... I suppose it's going to be candles and salads until the emergency services restore the utilities.'

Cameron continued to stare out of the empty window frame. But his thoughts kept coming back to the mysterious figure driving the psychedelic ice cream van through the stormy sky.

'It feels like nothing will ever be the same again,' he murmured.

'I know what you mean,' said Lulu, and as she turned around, her Elvis Presley memorial plate fell from its hook on the wall and crashed onto the floor, breaking into pieces.

CHAPTER TWO

TIME TO MOVE

'Nee-naww, neee-naww, nee-naww,' cried Cameron in his bedroom, imitating the sirens outside. They had filled the air with their persistent whine for days now as the emergency services went about their business, mending and patching up the destruction caused by the tornado.

The aftermath of the tornado had been difficult for them both. Pimple's council had asked people to stay in their homes while the terrible damage was cleared up. Friends and neighbours had rallied around bringing food parcels, emergency supplies and comfort but tempers were beginning to fray.

'Cameron, PLEASE stop it,' shouted Lulu from her bedroom. 'It's bad enough there's sirens outside, let alone in here.'

But Cameron couldn't help it. He was bored.

'Be a dear,' called Lulu, 'and plump the cushions on the sofa for me.'

Cameron wheeled his way down the hallway and thumped the cushions on the fake leopard skin sofa. Lulu had been cleaning all morning, getting everything in the flat in order. The newly repaired cocktail cabinet was sitting again in pride of place, its torn exterior neatly stitched with matching scarlet thread. A picture that had been blown across the room was back on its hook, albeit with a crack in the glass, and a new lampshade hung from the ceiling. The sitting room was beginning to look like home again.

The morning sun had made a sudden guest appearance from behind a grey cloud, its rays flooding the streets below with buttery yellow light, heralding a return to normality. Lulu and Cameron peered down at the streets below, bathing their faces in the welcome sunshine. People were starting to emerge. Traffic lights winked their intermittent colours for the first time in weeks, and rowdy children were letting off steam in the park.

Lulu reappeared at the entrance of the sitting room, threw open the door in a dramatic fashion and announced, 'We're going out!'

He took in his mum's colourful outfit. She was wearing a red polka dot dress with an enormous frill on the bottom and very high peep-toe shoes. She had put her hair up into a blue scarf, tied a bow in the front and was wearing a very elaborate pair of winged sunglasses.

'Great!' said Cameron, making his way over to the front door and grabbing the keys from the hall table. 'I was beginning to get cabin fever. Come on!'

'Happy in your chariot, Cameron?'

'*Carpe Diem*,' joked Cameron. He had started to refer to his chair as his chariot after finishing his summer holiday project about the Romans, and during his research he had picked up a few Latin words and phrases he was quite proud of. He liked to imagine himself as a Roman warrior entering the city triumphantly in a splendid golden chariot after a victorious battle. The last few weeks had certainly felt like a battle in more ways than one.

'Latin? You never stop surprising me,' marvelled Lulu as she collected the pieces of her beloved Elvis Presley memorial plate, wrapped them carefully in newspaper and placed them in her shopping bag.

'I'll take these into Alf Poppet's shop to be repaired. He'll make a good job of it.'

As they made their way out, Lulu grabbed their coats, turned and locked the door, rubbing her finger marks off the brass plate next to the doorframe, which read:

'HERE LIVES LULU SAINT-MILDRED-TUDOUR-MOLE-FLOUNCY-BIBBITT-McPHERSON and her son CAMERON TIBERIUS McPHERSON.'

Lulu's attachment to her surnames was one of

her little quirks. She told people that it made receptionists' jobs more interesting. She had married three times and had kept all her surnames, including her maiden name. Her first husband, Quentin Tudor-Mole, a musician, had divorced her on grounds of her being tone deaf. Her second husband, Ralph Flouncy-Bibbitt, an Arctic explorer, had more in common with seals and bears than with her and had never returned from the icy wastelands. Everyone assumed he had been some polar bear's breakfast. Her third husband, Cameron's father, had remarried but they remained on good terms. Pimple had a reputation for being an ordinary town, inhabited with eccentric people. Lulu was a fine example.

Lulu pushed Cameron down the narrow hallway toward the lift, the neon strip of lighting flickering above them. But as they approached the gated lift, their hearts sunk as they saw a lazily slung sign that read:

'BY ORDER OF THE MAGNIFICENT METROPOLIS OF PIMPLE WITH ADMISSION BY THE GREAT COUNCIL OF POTWELL AND THE WORKS DEPARTMENT OF TRICKLE-ON-TWEE.'

And then, in very small letters at the bottom of the sign, handwritten:

'THIS LIFT IS BROKEN UNTIL FURTHER NOTICE'.

CHAPTER THREE

NEXT-DOOR NEIGHBOUR

'CONKED OUT CRUMMY MACHINE!' yelled a frustrated Cameron on reading the sign.

His frustration was cut short on hearing the click of a latch, the sliding of a rusty long bolt, the rattling of an old chain and the turning of a squeaky lock. The door slowly opened and their inquisitive neighbour, Ruby Broomhead, appeared, bending her head to ensure that her mountain of white hair did not touch the top of the doorframe. Her pet brown mice, Inky and Poe, ran in and out of her powdered coiffure and swung from her cascading curls. She ducked through the door, sideways, in an enormous, hooped crinoline skirt. The skirt was red, white and blue, the colours of the French flag.

As she straightened herself, Cameron regarded her in all her barmy glory. Ruby Broomhead had a rather grand view of herself. Not in an arrogant way, more… delusional. She believed herself to be the reincarnation of Marie Antoinette, a French Queen who had been beheaded in a bloody revolution in 1793.

'Goodness gracious me, whatever's going on here?' said Ruby in a high-pitched, squeaky voice.

'Oh, Ruby, so sorry to disturb you, it's just the lift has broken down. We're desperate to get out and about. Especially today! Would you just mind looking after Cameron while I take the wheelchair down? Then I'll come back for him.'

'Certainly, my dear, but please don't be long, I've got to go out too. Inky and Poe have to take their exercise,' she said, spinning the large mouse wheel in her hair.

'Thanks, Ruby, I'm ever so grateful,' said Lulu.

Ruby ushered them into her pink and gold sitting room. It looked like an eighteenth-century French salon. In the middle of the room was a lilac chaise longue with a French flag draped over it.

Lulu picked Cameron up out of his wheelchair and laid him on the chaise, making him comfortable with various bolster cushions. She then folded the wheelchair into a more compact, moveable size.

'See you later, alligator,' said Lulu, calling behind her as she went down the stairs with the folded wheelchair.

'In a while, crocodile,' Cameron called after her.

'T.T.F.N,' said Ruby. She turned to Cameron. 'Ta ta for now,' she explained. 'Now, would you like a cupcake?'

Not the cakes again, thought Cameron to himself. He remembered the last cake she had made for him on his birthday. It had been completely inedible and he'd ended up throwing it out of his bedroom window. Even the seagulls had refused to eat it. But he remembered his mother's words: 'Always be polite to people... If possible.'

'Err... cupcakes... that would be lovely,' he replied.

Ruby popped into the kitchen and re-emerged with a plate of cupcakes that looked like rubble.

'Let's not forget Inky and Poe,' she said, removing the two mice from her hair and placing them on a side table. She broke one of the cupcakes in two and showered crumbs around them. 'They do so love my fantasy-in-vanilla cupcakes!'

Cameron tentatively picked up one of Ruby's culinary curiosities, wondering whether to take a few small, speculative mouthfuls, or just to shove it all in his mouth in one, to get it over and done with. He finally popped the entire thing into his mouth.

'Delicious, isn't it?' mumbled Ruby, stuffing a cupcake of her own into her mouth.

It tastes of sand and glue, thought Cameron. And the more he chewed, the thicker the texture became. He tried to swallow the gluey paste but it just stuck in his throat.

'Have you ever been on a parachute jump?' Ruby asked, quite out of the blue. 'You wouldn't need the lift then. You'd get down much quicker.'

'No,' gagged Cameron, 'but I'd like to try,' as he finally swallowed the remaining glutinous lump. 'But how's it going to work, you know, with me?'

'You're going to have to trust me, young man. You will be strapped to my back in a harness, and we shall make our grand descent from my bedroom window where the diving board is situated.'

'Okaaaay,' said Cameron, unsure but curious to find out more.

Ruby disappeared for a few minutes, then popped her head around the door, wearing aviator's glasses and a crash helmet which squashed her voluminous white hair out of the vents in the sides. Cameron started to giggle uncontrollably. It was all too absurd. Ruby placed a harness around his body and tied him to her back with a multitude of straps, buckles and bells.

'It's just like having a piggyback,' Cameron laughed.

'A flying piggy,' replied Ruby as they went into the bedroom. Cameron saw for the first time the enormous diving board, jutting out of the window next to her bed.

'Now, are you ready?'

Cameron thought about the last few days, cooped up in the apartment. He was ready for an adventure.

'Ready to rock and roll,' he said, adopting one of his mother's favourite phrases.

Ruby stared at the springboard in front of her and, taking deep rhythmical breaths, quickly strode the gangplank through the window, bounced and leapt into the air. The air rushed underneath the enormous hooped skirt, inflating the crinoline to capacity.

Cameron began to panic. Everything had happened so quickly.

'Ruby, pull the parachute cord!'

'There is no actual parachute,' replied a perfectly calm Ruby. 'The skirt *is* the parachute. You're perfectly safe.'

Cameron's heart was beating so fast he could hear it in his ears. But as he got used to the ride, his adrenalin slowed and the thrill of it overcame his fear. He could hear the bells on his harness tinkling and the wind whistling around his ears.

'Wheeeeeeeeeeeeeeeee!' he shouted at the top of his voice.

'Wonderful, isn't it,' shouted Ruby, 'to have the wind blowing around one's knickers!'

Lulu had been sitting in the forecourt of Grimthorpe Towers, taking a five-minute break in the wheelchair. Her eyes were closed as she tried to find the energy to walk up seventeen flights of stairs, pick up her son and carry him back down. She suddenly realised that her decision to go out was somewhat rash. How on earth would they get back up to the seventeenth floor if the lift wasn't repaired?

Her train of thought was broken by the sounds of tinkling bells and a woman and child laughing. She opened her eyes and looked up and saw the most extraordinary sight. With the sun glaring behind them, a pair of legs in long knickers slowly descended from the sky, a large parachute-like dress billowing around them. Lulu's jaw dropped open.

Ruby made a graceful landing on the grassy verge in front of her.

'There we are, my dear, one child safely delivered.'

For the first time in Lulu's life, she was stuck for something to say.

'We parachuted in! How cool is that!?' said Cameron, giving the thumbs up to Ruby.

'Here, let me help you,' said Lulu, walking over to unbuckle Cameron's harness and lift him back into his wheelchair.

'Honestly, Mum, that was fantastic!' said Cameron.

'Ruby, there are other ways of getting my son down the stairs,' chided Lulu, annoyed with Ruby for taking such a risk.

'Of course there are, my dear,' said Ruby, taking off her crash helmet, 'but none half as much fun. Now I must get on and see if the shops are open. One doesn't need a shopping basket when one has a crash helmet. It holds a bag of flour, six eggs and a pint of milk, all the ingredients one needs for "fantasy-in-vanilla" cupcakes. *Au revoir, mon Chérie, au revoir!*' And with no further ado, Ruby walked smartly down the path, swinging her crash helmet at her side as her hooped skirt bounced up and down and the bells jangled noisily on her harness.

'She is something else!' said Lulu, flabbergasted by her neighbour's cheek.

'*That* was something else!' shouted Cameron, as he and his mum made their way through Potwell Park and towards Alf Poppit's shop.

CHAPTER FOUR

A STRANGE ENCOUNTER

'You must get one of those dresses like Ruby's,' said Cameron enthusiastically as they meandered through Potwell Park. 'It would be very useful when the lift breaks down.'

'I'm assuming that your wheelchair would have its own parachute as well,' said Lulu dryly.

In the park, there were more signs of damage left by the tornado. An upturned car lay by the side of the lake, covered in thick green pondweed. It was next to a sign on a post which read:

'NO SWIMMING, DIVING OR BOATING. BEWARE! VERY DEEP WATER!'

'I must do something about taking swimming lessons,' decided Lulu, who had an absolute fear of anything to do with water, whether it was lakes, public baths or the sea. As if to warn her of the dangers, a large goose suddenly appeared from the inside of the car, hissing loudly. Thunder rumbled loudly overhead.

'Not again,' said Cameron.

Within seconds, the sound of a gentle pitter-patter became the gush of torrential rain, soaking them both in minutes.

'That's all we need,' said Lulu, pushing Cameron's chair. They hurried through the blinding rain and left the park through the nearest exit. Looking about them, they realised they had emerged onto a small road that was unfamiliar to them both. The rain continued to noisily pour down.

'Mum, let's get a taxi,' shouted Cameron.

'Easier said than done,' Lulu retorted. There were no taxis to be seen anywhere. 'Today *has* to get better!' she yelled.

'Look, there's a bus shelter over there. Let's take cover!' said Cameron.

Lulu pushed the wheelchair across the road, heading for the shelter. As she did so, the left back wheel got stuck in the metal grate of a drain. She pushed and pulled and heaved with all her might until, finally, the chair broke free – but to her dismay, she realised that the freed wheel was now bent out of shape. She struggled with the broken chair, managing to reach the bus shelter with Cameron still seated. They were now both flustered and utterly soaked.

'Now what?' said Cameron as he looked down at the twisted wheel, raindrops dripping from his wet hair into his lap.

'I'll call a taxi.' Lulu rummaged through her bag, took out her mobile phone and rang a number. No signal.

'Damn and blast and curse... stupid phone... stupid weather... stupid wheel,' ranted Lulu.

Cameron could just about see a row of houses past the long stone park wall. 'Maybe someone down there could help?'

'Well, I can't get any wetter!' said Lulu and with that she set off. 'Stay put! Don't talk to strangers, and if you need help, just shout.'

Cameron watched his mum walk down the road. Ten minutes went by without a sign of anyone on the deserted street. But the rain started to peter out and the dark clouds began to move on. The sun burst out like a buttercup. The street was strangely quiet. Cameron felt like he was the only person left in the world. No cars or buses drove by. No people walked past. It was only him and the sound of dripping rain. He looked up and watched a large raindrop fall to the ground in slow motion. It splashed into a puddle at his feet, filling it with an explosion of colours.

'Weird...'

His nostrils twitched. He could smell strawberries and cream, bubblegum and apple pie, freshly baked double choc chip cookies, caramel sundaes and banana split. He looked up, following the colours as they arched up into the sky, forming a perfect rainbow.

'I'm at the end of a rainbow. Even more weird...'

In the distance, at the far end of the rainbow, he could see something coming towards him. The dark splodge got bigger and bigger as it came nearer. Cameron was mesmerised by it.

And then, all at once, he knew what it was.

'It's the ice cream van from the tornado!'

It looked like a bashed-about 1960s Volkswagen camper van. It was painted pink and sky-blue with a light green trim around the doors and windows. Enormous round headlights flashed orange and purple. The exhaust pipe was twisted like knotted rope and disgorged thick purple smoke that smelled of toffee and pineapple.

The van slid down the end of the rainbow highway, slashed through the puddle and came to a halt near the bus shelter, shaking and shuddering as the engine puffed and wheezed. At the back of the van was a silver spiral staircase that led to an upper deck surrounded by battlements embossed with suns, moons and stars.

Emblazoned on the side of the van in colourful letters were the words:

'MR PEA'S INTER-GALACTIC DREAM FACTORY.'

A very tall man climbed out of the driver's seat.

He had long pepper-grey dreadlocks, decorated with silver shells and odd-shaped beads that glowed against his black skin. His lively, friendly eyes were as green as mint and his wide mouth beamed end to end with a sparkling smile.

'Hello, Cameron,' said the man, in a soft Caribbean accent.

'How do you know my name?'

'I know lots of things, little fella,' he said, extending a large hand. 'By the way, I'm Mr Pea.'

'Hello, Mr Pea,' said Cameron. 'That's a funny name.'

'Well it's *shorter* than Cameron Tiberius McPherson. Now *that's* a mouthful!' Mr Pea chuckled.

Cameron looked at this man curiously. He seemed to know an awful lot. He wore bright orange overalls, embroidered with suns, moons, planets and stars. Around his waist was a wide sturdy brown leather belt with strange-looking tools hanging off it. These were not tools to be found in the usual hardware stores of Pimple.

'Are you a mechanic?' quizzed Cameron.

'Nearly right. Actually I'm a MAGANIC. I make and repair things. Now, what have we got here?' He knelt in front of Cameron, placing his large hands on the front wheels of the chair. 'A broken chariot?'

Then in his soft, friendly voice, Mr Pea started to rap:

'A broken dream may need a fixin',
In my van I'll do the mixin'.
I'll oil your wish and make it work,
I'll clean your dream of all its dirt.
So come on board, no time to waste!
Create your dream with fun and haste.
Your wheelchair's broken, well don't panic.
I'm Mr Pea the whizz Maganic.'

Cameron was lost for words. 'The Inter Ga... Gal... lactic Dream Factory?' he managed eventually, reading the letters on the side of the van. 'Can I go inside?'

'Be my guest, little fella,' said Mr Pea. He picked up Cameron in his strong arms and carried him into the dream factory.

'Wow!' exclaimed Cameron. The inside of the van was as big as Cameron's sitting room at home. It was much bigger on the inside than it was on the outside.

But that's impossible, he thought.

Mr Pea carried Cameron over to a big yellow sofa and placed him gently down. It felt soft and squishy like furry jelly. As soon as Cameron relaxed into it, it moulded itself around him, supporting both his neck and back. Something began to tickle.

'Whooaah, what's that?' He giggled. The sofa continued to tickle him, under his arms, behind his ears, under his chin and all of his ticklish places.

Mr Pea gave Cameron a big grin.

'Whenever you're low,
Or been in a pickle,
What gets you laughin',
Is a mighty big tickle!'

Cameron noticed a big blue button on the arm of the sofa.

'What does this do?' he asked Mr Pea. Not waiting for an answer, he pushed it. The sofa immediately stopped tickling him, letting out the most extraordinary burping noise as it did so.

'Would you like a drink from the Think Drink machine?' Mr Pea asked, walking over to a bright red vending machine, full of rainbow-coloured cans.

'What's that?' said Cameron, puzzled.

'Focus on a colour and then let's see what happens,' said Mr Pea. He rummaged around in his pockets, found a token and popped it in the vending slot. A can of Think Drink rumbled out of the machine. Mr Pea pulled off the metal ring and handed the fizzy drink to Cameron.

'There you go.'

Cameron took the drink and tried to decide on a colour. He stared at the bright red vending machine. Suddenly his taste buds were blasted with the taste of red fruit, the sweetness of strawberries and raspberries, the tartness of redcurrants and rhubarb and the luscious juice of pomegranates. He took another gulp and then looked at the blue button on the arm of the sofa. An explosion of blackberries, blueberries and blackcurrants hit his palate.

'I like this!' Cameron enthused, shaking his can to see how much he had left.

'Look into my eyes, little fella,' teased Mr Pea.

Mr Pea's bright green eyes were one of the first things Cameron had noticed about his new friend.

Green… like vegetables, he thought to himself as he looked at Mr Pea's eyes and took the last swig of his Think Drink. His mouth filled with the taste of cabbage and spinach.

'*Uuuugghh!*' he hollered.

> '*Delicious and good are most things green,*
> *be good to your body, don't be mean!*'

Mr Pea rapped as he walked over to his workbench. He picked up a silver helmet that looked like a motorcyclist's crash helmet. All around the middle were strange-looking hieroglyphics, usually found on the walls of ancient Egyptian pyramids. And sprouting from the top were glass antennae. 'Now let's get down to business,' he said as he sat down on the sofa next to Cameron.

'What on earth is that?'

'This, little fella, is the one and only dream machine,' said Mr Pea in a reverential whisper.

'Oooh... what does it do?' asked Cameron.

'It extracts your dreams, even the most hidden ones,' said Mr Pea, carefully placing the silver helmet on Cameron's head. 'All you have to do is close your eyes, sit back and relax while the machine does its ting.'

Cameron closed his eyes. He could feel a slight vibration from the helmet's antennae.

'Clear your head of worldly thoughts and focus your mind's eye. Beyond the dark lies the light,' said Mr Pea mysteriously.

At first there was complete darkness as Mr Pea had foretold, but then a dim pulsating light appeared behind a hazy mist. The light throbbed brighter and brighter. And from far away, he could hear a dim beat.

'Look into the light,' said Mr Pea, his voice fading away.

The light was now a dazzling white. He could hear the beat of military drums and the blast of horns.

What's going on? Cameron thought.

He heard a shout out of the mist. 'Cameron! Cameron!'

He looked down and saw his own fist, tightly gripping a pair of leather reins. Looking ahead, he could see the reins attached to four magnificent black stallions. He could feel a leather strap under his chin. Putting his hand to his head, he could feel a heavy helmet, a metal helmet embossed with what felt like a bird. He lifted his head upwards. The mist cleared to reveal a row of dignitaries seated on a balcony, saluting him.

'Cameron! Cameron!'

The roar of the crowd filled his ears. A garland of flowers thrown by one of the crowd fell into the chariot. Cameron looked down. Past his bronze breast plate, now gleaming in the sun; past his purple toga embroidered with gold, he could see... clearly... that he was standing... independently... on his own two feet.

Chapter Five

THE GOLDEN CHAIR

As Lulu walked down the road looking for help, she had that feeling, particular to mothers, that something wasn't quite right with her child. She had been walking for about ten minutes and hadn't been able to find anyone. The streets were deserted. There was no one to help. And *that* feeling just wouldn't go away.

'I'm going back,' she decided, doing a roundabout turn and hurrying back toward the bus shelter.

From a distance, she could just make out an odd-looking lustrous shape behind the glass side-panel of the bus shelter. As she got nearer, she could see it was a chair – and a golden chair to boot, almost a chariot! 'What the...' she said, as she approached the chair.

Cameron was sitting, slumped in the golden wheelchair. He was fast asleep and softly snoring. Lulu grabbed his arm and gently shook it.

'Wakey, wakey, Cam...'

Cameron opened his eyes. His mum's face was right up close to his, her large luminous eyes blue and concerned.

'How are you feeling, Cameron? Are you all right?' said Lulu.

He stretched his arms in the air and yawned loudly.

'I'm fine,' he said sleepily.

'And why, young man, are you sitting in this? I'm not sure what it is... this strange chair?'

What strange chair is that? thought Cameron, yawning again. As he woke, he was starting to take on board what his mother was saying. He looked down. His arms were resting on what seemed to be the top of carved golden wings. The seat he was sitting in was luxuriously padded in purple.

'Whoah!' he exclaimed. This was definitely NOT his wheelchair!

'Answers, young man! Where did you get this from?' said Lulu, trying to get her son's attention for more than a few seconds.

'It really is like a Roman chariot...' said Cameron out loud, not really listening to his mother. He leaned forward and noticed that on either side of the seat were two golden sphinxes forming the chair's front panels.

'Who gave you this chair?' demanded Lulu.

Cameron saw his mum's mouth moving but didn't hear a word. He was too preoccupied with all the details of his new chair. His feet were resting on a scroll-shaped footrest. Hanging above his head and supported by a golden rod was a Roman centurion's plumed helmet, crowned with two short glass antennae. He leant over to check out the wheels. They were strong and sturdy and had spokes just like the wheels on a chariot. 'Awesome,' he said running his fingers down them. 'So it wasn't a dream, it was all real! Mr Pea really does exist!'

'Mr Pea? Mr PEA? Who is Mr Pea and what is this... contraption? CAMERON, ARE YOU LISTENING TO ME?' snapped Lulu.

'I wonder how it works?' said Cameron. On the right arm of the chair, in what appeared to be a control panel, were four buttons. One was purple, one orange, one pink and the other green.

'Hold on a minute!' exclaimed Lulu. 'We don't know what they do.'

'Only one way to find out,' replied Cameron decisively. But before he could touch any of the buttons, the two antennae above his head whizzed around, making a high-pitched whirr. The golden chair lurched forward.

'Wow, I didn't touch anything. I only thought about it,' cried Cameron in disbelief.

'Maybe that's how it works?' said Lulu. 'Why don't you think something else?'

Cameron thought about going around in a circle. The antennae whirred again and the chair dutifully rotated in a perfect smooth circle. 'It's just like the Think Drink machine!' he yelled. 'Whatever I think, it does.' The chair circled back over to where Lulu was standing.

'I wonder what this does?' said Cameron. He was just about to press the purple button when Lulu grabbed his hand away. 'That's enough, my boy!'

'Mum!' cried Cameron, annoyed, slamming his right hand down in a temper on the other side of the chair. In doing so, the breast of one of the sphinxes fell open and a scroll of paper fell onto the pavement.

Cameron and Lulu looked at each other. 'What is happening today!?' exclaimed Lulu.

The scroll started to vibrate on the floor, making a low humming noise. Suddenly it rocketed into the air with a tremendous WHOOSH, thirty metres up into the sky. There it exploded into a multitude of golden letters, which fell to form words, right in front of their eyes.

And the words began to sing:

> *'Release the magic in your heart.*
> *It's all inside, it's where you start.*

Desires and dreams will help you move.
You'll run, you'll fly, you'll dance life's groove.
Think hard 'bout what you'll achieve,
In helping others when in need.
So make your wish, count ten to zero,
Believe in you and be the HERO!'

As quickly as they had appeared, the singing words evaporated in a cloud of fizzling sparks.

'I... but... it's... what... I...' Cameron couldn't quite get the words out.

Lulu knelt down and held Cameron's hands. 'What exactly happened while I was away? You need to tell me, Cameron, so I can begin to understand what we're dealing with here.'

Cameron told Lulu about all the extraordinary events that had happened to him while she'd been away, from Mr Pea's arrival down the rainbow highway, to his extraordinary dream of being a Roman general.

Lulu was even more bewildered than ever by her son's story. 'Sounds to me as if you had an encounter with an alien or a wizard... or something.'

'A MAGANIC, actually. Mr Pea makes and repairs MAGICAL things,' Cameron explained, touching the arms of his sparkling new chair with pride.

'Well, Cameron, I can't say I understand it. But it's time to come back down to earth,' said Lulu, pointing to the broken plate in her bag. 'Come on, let's get this fixed.' And she escorted Cameron in his new golden chair towards Alf Poppet's shop.

CHAPTER SIX

ROCKIN' AND A ROLLIN'

The sign above Alf Poppet's shop read: 'ALF'S REPAIR SHOP – POP-IT-IN-BROKEN, PICK-IT-UP-SMOKIN''

Lulu and Cameron peered in through the old paned glass of the curious shop. It was crammed full of all manner of things, from the mundane to the exotic. There were irons and buckets, huge shells and coloured fans, very old televisions and glittering crystal glasses, stuffed toys with one eye and ornate candlesticks, dusty books, dolls with smashed heads, broken bicycles and old lampshades. Behind the cluttered, cobwebbed windowpanes and the collection of curios, sitting on a stool at the far end of the shop, was Mr Poppet himself. He was looking through a magnifying glass at the workings of a very old watch. As Lulu and Cameron pushed the door open, they were greeted by a cacophony of ringing bells. It reminded Lulu of her three wedding days.

Mr Poppet looked up and put the magnifying glass down. He put on his own circular brown glasses. They had bottle lenses. Cameron thought he looked like an enormous owl.

'You frightened the life out of me!' said Mr Poppet.

Cameron loved going to Mr Poppet's shop. It was an Aladdin's cave, full of the most curious objects. There was always something extraordinary to look at.

'Well, if it isn't Lulu and young Cameron,' he said, looking Cameron's chair up and down. 'My my, that's quite a piece of machinery. I've never seen the likes of it before. Is it new?'

'Yes, it is, and it's magic!' exclaimed Cameron, hardly able to contain himself.

'Tragic? What's tragic about it? It looks fine to me,' said Mr Poppet.

'MAGIC!' Cameron and Lulu giggled in unison.

'I'm sorry, my hearing isn't what it used to be.' Mr Poppet smiled, winking at Cameron. 'Magic, eh? Well, we won't need to repair it then. So what can I do for you?'

'This fell off the wall,' Lulu explained, handing the broken pieces of the plate to Alf.

'That storm has been good for business. So many broken things.'

'It was my favourite Elvis Presley plate,' said Lulu ruefully.

'Well, in that case,' said Mr Poppet, 'I might have just the thing for you.' And with that he disappeared behind the counter for a few minutes and reappeared with a vinyl record. He placed it on an old record player, switched it on and turned the volume up. 'The very best of Elvis, in honour of your visit.'

'That is so very kind of you,' murmured Lulu appreciatively. As the music started to take hold, she began to click her fingers and tap her feet. She shook her head from side to side and wiggled her hips. Taking hold of the handles of Cameron's wheelchair, Lulu started to move it to the beat of the music.

'You don't need to do that, Mum, I can do it myself,' said Cameron. The antennae on the helmet started to whirr again as the chair spun around to the left and then to the right, performing a figure of eight.

'This is great!'

Cameron thought about the chair going backwards and forwards and as he did so the chair reacted in tune with his thoughts.

'Cool!' He had never danced on his own before. He closed his eyes and listened to the music.

'*Let's rock, everybody, let's rock,*' sung Elvis from the record player.

Cameron could feel the music flowing through him. He was getting so caught up in it. He felt one of the panel's buttons throb under his hand. He opened his eyes and saw the purple button pulsing with light. He caught his reflection in a mirror on the wall. He could see the whirring, buzzing antennae on his helmet changing colour, flickering as they spun around and around. But all he could think about was dancing... jiving and dancing... *dancing*.

I want to DANCE like ELVIS, he thought as he raised his hand and slammed it down hard on the pulsing purple button.

A flash of intense light filled the room and spun the chair around in what looked like a golden tornado. Lulu and Mr Poppet screamed in shock. Things like this didn't happen in Alf's repair shop!

Cameron's chair spun round and round in a sparkling whirlwind. He felt his body being lifted by a supernatural force of energy. Suddenly he wasn't *sitting* in his chair anymore. He was suspended in mid-air. Then the strangest thing happened. *WHOOSH!* He was standing erect. He felt something clamp onto his legs as they straightened. It felt like armour.

Cameron couldn't quite believe what was happening. His chair was changing shape before his very eyes. He felt a strange sensation like something was melting around him. The intense light started to dim. Gradually it ebbed away.

Cameron found himself sitting in a pair of huge mechanical legs with flared trousers. The helmet had changed into a golden quiff and the wings on the side of the chair had transformed into a large upturned collar. It was an Elvis dancing machine!

Cameron's wish had come true.

Cameron remembered from his mum's collection of Elvis films how the King had danced. His whole body seemed to be reacting to the rhythm and beat of the music. He couldn't believe how different his legs felt. He started to tentatively move them. It felt a little weird at first, a little wobbly, but he kept thinking of all Elvis' moves. Soon he was gyrating his hips, bravely strutting his body forward. How cool it was to dance!

'Whoah! These new legs of mine are a beast!' he exclaimed, checking out the details of his new mechanical legs. The four coloured buttons now formed the studs on a wide gilded belt with the sphinxes' faces as the central buckle. The legs were a golden metallic colour and embellished either side with embossed wings.

'This is just like one of my old Transformer toys!' cried Cameron. He jumped in the air and spread his legs apart, keeping one of them straight while the other quivered and shimmied. He thrust his hips forward and the whole movement resonated through his body. He gyrated his hips and wiggled his upper body in a back shimmy, swaggering his body forward, doing the Cool Bird Strut. He knocked his knees together and then jumped his legs apart again. He couldn't believe what his legs were doing. He only had to think of a dance move and his legs responded.

'The KING is in the HOUSE!' he yelled jubilantly, spreading out his arms just like Elvis. He twisted and turned and strutted all around the shop.

Lulu was dumbstruck for the second time that day and Mr Poppet stood as motionless as a statue. Both of them were wondering what to do next.

'Number forty-seven said to number three, you're the cutest jailbird I ever did see, I sure would be delighted with your company, come on and do the jailhouse rock with me,' crooned Elvis out of the record player.

Cameron grabbed hold of Lulu's hand and started to jive. He had never *actually* jived before but, somehow, his legs knew what to do. *1-2-rock-a-step, 3-4-triple-step. They chasséd to the left, they chasséd to the right;* he let go of her hand and she spun around like a spinning top, collapsing dizzily onto a pile of Persian rugs.

Cameron couldn't believe he was dancing like Elvis. He felt wonderful. He felt like the King of Rock and Roll!

Mr Poppet came out from behind the counter, laughing and clapping his hands to the music. He grabbed Cameron by the hand, all the time whooping and singing along. Lulu sang along too, out of tune, in her usual dog-like howl.

Cameron was exhausted. His body wasn't used to such vigorous activity and he thought it best that he should rest up for a while. He sort of remembered something Lulu had said, about having too much of a good thing – but after all, this was only his first time. He looked down at his ornate buckle belt and saw the pink button was now a gently pulsating light. Without hesitating, he pressed it.

There was another enormous flash of intense golden light as the whole shop seemed to spin around him. Again he felt himself suspended in mid-air, and there was a strange sensation all around his legs as if they were melting. *WHOOSH!* He was falling backwards at super speed. Falling… falling… falling… Then everything was still.

He opened his eyes. He was sitting in his golden chair again. Relief. He quickly checked everything was where it should be. The helmet was still above his head. The sphinxes were in front and the golden wings at the side. His feet were resting comfortably on the scroll-shaped footrest.

'Well, that certainly works!' said an amazed Lulu, getting up from the pile of Persian carpets and brushing herself down. 'Are you all right, Cameron?'

'I feel great!' said Cameron, beaming from ear to ear. 'That was brilliant, Mum! Isn't dancing awesome!?'

'Fantastic,' wheezed Mr Poppet. 'I've seen some things in my life but that takes the biscuit! You'd better be careful with that chair of yours, lad. There's some mighty magic there.'

'Mighty magic indeed, Mr Poppet!'

CHAPTER SEVEN

THE STRANGE RESTAURANT

'Phew, all that dancing has made me hungry,' said Cameron exhaustedly. 'My tummy's rumbling.'

'Mine too,' agreed Lulu. 'After this morning, I think we need to sit down, eat something and take stock. I'd like to at least get through lunch without any further surprises.'

They said their goodbyes to Mr Poppet and left the shop, the three bells ringing behind them. Walking down Pimple's High Street, they went in search of somewhere to eat. Restaurant after restaurant was closed or undergoing repairs because of the storm. They walked past a café covered in scaffolding, where workmen were replacing the roof. Elsewhere, windows were boarded up. Nothing seemed to be open.

They eventually came to the Assembly buildings, Pimple's council's headquarters. It was a large grey stone building with eight arched windows and Palladian classical pillars on either side of a big heavy-panelled door. Opposite this elegant building lay leafy gardens, fenced in behind wrought iron railings. The gate leading to the gardens was an intricate design of wrought iron flowers and insects. On either side of the gate were two carved stone pillars, crowned with metal coronets on top of which perched two stone vultures facing one another.

'I think there's a café in there,' said Lulu hesitantly, 'but I don't know anyone who's been.'

'Come on then, let's give it a try,' said Cameron.

'We can't. This is Gitwick Gardens, and look, it says private.'

'Well, the gate is open. Anyway, it doesn't say it's private.'

'It does! There's a sign on the gate… Look.'

'No, that sign says "RIVATE",' said a sharp-eyed Cameron, 'and I don't know what "rivate" means, do you?'

'You've got a point there,' replied Lulu.

They crossed the road. The gate had been left open, its large padlock dangling from a chain. As Lulu and Cameron pushed the heavy gates open, the hinges made a loud squeaking noise. The gate led onto a winding path that snaked its way around the edge of the gardens, before directing them to the centre. Luscious thick green bushes and plants grew in the borders and weeping birch trees with low hanging, pendulous branches brushed Lulu's shoulders as they walked down the path. To the left and right, gardeners were clearing up broken branches and boughs, debris from the great storm.

'I feel like a trespasser,' whispered Lulu as a gentle breeze blew through the trees.

'Look over there,' said Cameron, pointing to the top of a domed roof, peeping above the treetops and glimmering in the sunlight. They quickened their pace towards the promise of something to eat.

At the end of the pathway stood a magnificent glass building that had miraculously escaped the storm. The building was octagonal in shape, a masterpiece of engineering, its glass panels shooting toward the sky then curving outward like a shimmering crystal flower.

'Wow, impressive,' said Cameron, as they made their way toward the end of the path and approached the front of the building. He could just make out some letters in stained glass above the magnificent entrance.

'EPI-CURI-OSITY CAFÉ,' said Cameron, reading the words aloud.

'Come on, I'm ravenous,' said Lulu, pushing open the glass door.

A coat check girl looked up from her book and sprang from her seat.

'Good afternoon. Lovely day, isn't it?' said Lulu cheerfully, as she handed over their coats. The girl took them but said nothing.

'Lights are on but nobody's at home,' muttered Lulu to herself.

As Lulu and Cameron turned away, the girl threw their coats on the floor behind her, sat right back down and carried on reading.

Lulu and Cameron made their way into the main part of the restaurant. The smell of sickly perfume hit them the moment they walked in.

'Phew, what a pong!' said Cameron.

To the left and right were two enormous stained-glass friezes like cathedral windows. The one to the left of them depicted a panda and a tiger in a race towards a great bubbling pot. The one to the right depicted a dolphin, a whale and a rare and extinct fish swimming frantically toward an enormous silver hook dangling in the water.

The restaurant was a hive of activity, with waiters rushing to-and-fro between two distinctly different sets of people. The two groups were the Hoity-Toitys and the La-Di-Das, the two opposing parties in the Assembly that governed Pimple.

These two groups were as different to one another as chalk and cheese. On the left, at purple-coloured tables, sat the Hoity-Toitys. They were an opinionated lot with loud voices and gravelly guffaws. As far as *they* were concerned, all mammals were for wearing and eating. So the Hoity-Toitys ate them. Or at least anything that ran. The women sat there in their enormous fur coats, even in summer, while the gentlemen wore hunting hats and tweed. In Assembly meetings, they would bellow their opinions out loudly, shouting over their opponents with their noisy and thunderous points of view.

On the right, at green-coloured tables, sat the La-Di-Das. They were an argumentative bunch with screeching voices and nasal laughter. As far as *they* were concerned, all fish were for catching and eating. So the La-Di-Das ate them. Or at least anything that swam. The women sat there in their scanty slippery silks and satins, even in winter, while the gentlemen wore mackintoshes and waders. In Assembly meetings, they would screech their protestations, drowning out their opponents with shrill and piercing points of views.

Surveying the proceedings from a lofty, eagle-fashioned pulpit stood Monsieur Grandee Cornichon, the manager of the establishment. Perched on his head, slightly skew-whiff, sat an ill-fitting toupee. And on either side of his great hooked nose were two beady bird-like eyes with which he slowly fixed his unflinching gaze on Cameron.

'Scary man at 3 o'clock,' said Cameron. Lulu looked to the right and clocked the vulture-like manager in his nest. She felt goosebumps prickle on her arms.

'Can I 'elp you at all?' sneered Monsieur Cornichon.

'We'd like something to eat,' said Lulu, recoiling as his chilling eyes looked straight through her.

'You can't have *zat* wheelchair in *zis* restaurant,' spat Monsieur Cornichon, pointing to Cameron's wheelchair.

'It's my chariot,' said Cameron defiantly.

Monsieur Cornichon clicked his fingers and from behind a nearby door appeared Paloma Snuck, the diminutive assistant manager. Two cones of red frizzy hair framed her round face, and she had a small upturned nose that was perpetually stuck up in the air. She waddled towards the pulpit's stairs, her feet turned out like a ballerina's, dismissing Lulu and Cameron with a haughty glance as she passed. Upon reaching the top of the pulpit, she heralded her arrival by slamming an enormous reservation book down onto the lectern, before Monsieur Cornichon.

'Get ze child and its mother OUT of my restaurant,' hissed Monsieur Cornichon, through his jagged teeth. 'She 'as terrible clothes on and zat wheelchair will make 'orrible marks over my perfectly polished floor.'

'I'm afraid, Madame, we are fully booked, so unfortunately we're unable to accommodate you,' announced Paloma imperiously.

'Fully booked, eh? I can count at least three vacant tables. Besides...' Lulu pointed at another empty table situated at the back of the restaurant. 'It's two o'clock. Surely there can't be that many people coming for lunch now. What about over there?'

'That... er... um... table is... er... reserved for Lord and Lady Limpid-Smythe. Yes, that's right... Lord and Lady Slimpid-Lythe at two o'clock.'

A frustrated Lulu grabbed the book from Paloma Snuck's hands and opened the pages at today's date. Running her fingers down the page, she announced, 'I used to be a manageress in a restaurant myself, and I can see from the page in front of me that there is NO reservation for Limpid-Smythe. In fact, your last reservation was at 1.20! So a very hungry little boy and I would like something to eat!'

Monsieur Grandee Cornichon glared at Paloma. She had not handled the situation to his satisfaction at all. There was a very awkward silence between the two of them as they continued to stare at one another, each waiting for the other to resolve the issue.

Lulu interrupted the silence. 'Do you know who I am?' she said regally. 'I am the widow of Ralph Flouncy-Bibbitt, the Arctic explorer.'

A look of recognition swept over Monsieur Cornichon's face. He remembered reading the story in the newspaper.

'Ah yes, I remember zis story, very interesting. 'E was eaten by a polar bear, *non*?'

'Conjecture, monsieur, pure conjecture,' dismissed Lulu, who had had quite enough. 'Now, can we have a table, please?'

'Miss Snuck, show Mrs Flouncy-Bibbitt to ze table,' said a reluctant Monsieur Cornichon, conceding defeat. He could see they were not to be deterred.

'*Actually*, my mum's name is Mrs Lulu Saint-Mildred-Tudor-Mole-Flouncy-Bibbitt-McPherson,' pronounced Cameron to the bewildered manager. 'And *my* name is Cameron Tiberius McPherson,' he added triumphantly.

It wasn't easy for Cameron to negotiate his chair through the restaurant. The dining floor was crammed full of tables and chairs, and everyone was far too busy to move: far too busy stuffing their mouths with food or guzzling large glasses of wine or thumping their fists on the table or whispering juicy bits of gossip. Or far too short-tempered at the inconvenience of being required to. Cameron's polite excuse me-s were rebuffed with outraged replies of 'Do we *have* to?' or 'We're having our lunch,' or 'Wheelchairs to be left in the car park!'

Cameron found it all quite unpleasant: the chewing mouths, the crinkly throats, the loud shouting, the yapping pet miniature dogs, the waiters weaving in and around the tables with enormous silver trays, balanced dangerously on one hand.

The round Hoity-Toity gentlemen all had brown skin as tough and shiny as newly polished leather boots. Their moustaches and beards were stained with the blood of the meat as they bellowed and barked at the staff. The plump Hoity-Toity ladies all wore round black sunglasses and had blank orange faces devoid of any expression. Their throats were covered in rubies, all of them as large as foil-wrapped sweets. Diamond tiaras sparkled from the top of their blue-black hair. Their greasy fingers crammed chunks of bloody red meat into their greedy mouths. Seeing their fur coats hunched up around their shoulders, Cameron was reminded of hyenas feeding.

Yuk! he thought.

The La-Di-Das were a different kettle of fish. The men's complexions were as pale as ivory and their eyes were glassy green. They screeched shrill opinions at each other and screamed at the staff. The women's skin was as translucent as silvery fish. Their thin, pale throats dripped with sapphires and diamond fascinators twinkled from their tight bleached hair. Their skinny fingers dangled slivers of slimy fish down their greedy throats.

They look like a shoal of mackerel, thought Cameron, as he watched them in their slippery silks and reflective silver sunglasses.

The officious Paloma Snuck led Cameron and Lulu through the seated guests until they arrived at a small table at the back of the restaurant near to the swinging kitchen doors. She stood with one hand on her hip and glared at them both, oblivious to their difficulties navigating through the restaurant.

She was just about to leave when she heard Monsieur Cornichon loudly announcing the arrival of a VIP. She stood to attention next to Cameron.

'Her Unctuousness ze Pearl of Pimple and ze Very Meddling Sniveller of Witter-On-Next-the-Sea!'

All the Hoity-Toitys and La-Di-Das stood up and reverentially bowed their heads.

'What's a Pearl?' asked Cameron, tugging Paloma's sleeve.

'Oh really,' said Paloma Snuck indignantly. 'The Pearl is the JEWEL of Pimple!' And with that, she stuck her nose higher in the air and flounced off.

Cameron watched the VIPs walking towards him. The Pearl wore an enormous headdress, covered in every kind of summer flower. Two assistants stood either side of her, holding silver poles which propped up the enormous construction, while a little boy ran in front of her, squeezing a gilded atomiser so that every sniff of air she breathed was perfumed. Cameron stared at her taut pale skin and her perfect tombstone teeth.

'Mum, why does she look like all the other women?' he whispered.

Lulu giggled. 'They've probably all been to the same plastic surgeon.'

'And why does she wear that funny hat?'

'That's her hat of office. She's the leader of the Assembly that governs Pimple. Though why she has all those airs and graces is beyond me. She was once an air hostess.'

Behind the Pearl walked the Meddling Sniveller, a stout man dressed in an orange cassock. His face was as red and round as a tomato, and around his neck he wore an enormous chain of office set with purple stones. He held a large orange, studded with cloves, which he occasionally stooped to sniff. He stopped and peered at Cameron through a pair of silver binoculars.

'Poor boy,' he pronounced loudly, with affected sympathy, and placing his orange next to his nose, he inhaled and moved on.

'What was that all about?' quizzed Cameron.

'He's the Meddling Sniveller, the Pearl's spiritual and astrological advisor. Apparently he's the bore of the century,' whispered Lulu.

The Pearl of Pimple and the Meddling Sniveller glided towards a raised platform. Their attendants fussed around them as they sat underneath a silken canopy. Monsieur Cornichon clicked his fingers and growled, 'CHAMPAGNE!' and the waiting staff rushed around like worker ants attending their Queen.

'How is she going to eat her lunch with that big funny hat on her head?' asked Cameron, captivated by the Pearl and her entourage. They were too funny for words!

An oversized menu was suddenly placed in front of Cameron and Lulu by an ungracious Paloma Snuck, blocking their view of the Pearl. 'The menu!' she announced rudely, and with that she flounced off again.

Distracted from the Pearl and her entourage, Lulu and Cameron both looked with wonder at the exotic menu in front of them.

ENTRÉES
Ravioli of Crocodile
Salad of Crispy Bat Wings
Tempura of Fish Eyes
Squid Ink Surprise

MAINS
Bleeding steak of Bison
Roast Rump of Camel (Rare)
Spiced Meaty Entrails

Live Slithery Slime Fish
Grilled Sea Eel with Sautéed Sponges
Curried Fish Guts

DESSERT
Duck Pond Pudding
Sardine Ice Cream
Liquorice Roly-Poly Pudding with Greeney
   Custard
Stinging Nettle Pancakes with Syrup of Figs
A Selection of Ripened Cheeses

'Absolutely disgusting,' mumbled Lulu under her breath.

'Yuk!' exclaimed Cameron.

'There's nothing here I would ever want to eat,' said Lulu. 'I think we'd better stick to the cheeses. Now where's that infuriating woman gone?'

Cameron was busy looking around to find Paloma when he was distracted by a flurry of activity from a nearby table. Some of the Hoity-Toitys and the La-Di-Das had left their separate tables and joined each other at one large shared table. They were gathered around one individual. Cameron could just make out a man's striped jacket. But who was he? And what on earth was bringing these two groups together? One of the Hoity-Toity gentlemen clicked his fingers and a waiter rushed over to rearrange the chairs. As the gathered group parted to make way, Cameron could finally see who everyone had come to watch.

Holding court sat Erikson Longfingers. He was a tall thin man with a straw boater on his head and a striped blazer with a yellow dandelion in the buttonhole.

Cameron watched curiously as the man brought out a pack of cards. He dexterously shuffled them, amusing his attentive audience with a display of tricks that had them all laughing and whooping with delight. He made an extravagant concertina with the cards before packing them away in an inside pocket. Silence fell around the table. He raised his elegant hands in the air, fluttering his fingers and plucking the air as if playing an invisible harp.

'He's hypnotising the people around him,' said an astonished Lulu. The spectators' eyes widened and glazed as their mouths drooped and dribbled. Everyone around Erikson Longfingers seemed dazzled, dumbfounded, frozen in time. No one noticed that, while one hand was mid-air, the other was darting in and out of his audience's elaborate clothing. Cameron wondered what on earth he was up to.

Erikson Longfingers felt that particular sense of someone watching him. He turned his head, narrowed his sly, snake eyes and fixed his gaze on

Cameron. Had that nosey little boy sitting in the peculiar wheelchair seen his crafty business?

I'll just give him a little scare, he thought to himself. He placed his long, bony forefinger on his chest, then two fingers under his eyes, before pointing dramatically at Cameron, mouthing, 'I'm-watching-you.'

Cameron shuddered as he realised what the nasty looking man was saying to him. 'Urggh!'

'What did you say?' inquired Lulu, who herself had been momentarily transfixed by the hypnotist and his tricks.

Erikson Longfingers suddenly clicked his fingers and everyone around him came out of their trance, carrying on as if nothing had happened. He rose from the table and, after shaking the gentlemen's hands and kissing the ladies' fingers, stood for a brief moment before thrusting his right hand into his jacket. Pulling out a white dove, he threw it into the air with a flourish. Everyone applauded and cooed with amazement as they watched the bird fly up into the vaulted heights of the crystal dome. Leaving the table, he passed through the crowded restaurant, all the time intently regarding Cameron and his mother from the corner of his eye.

'Ze spectacular, ze magical Erikson Longfingerrrrs!' announced Monsieur Cornichon.

The magician made his way to the reception area

to the sound of rapturous applause. Cameron continued to watch him closely. He wasn't quite sure what it was but there was something very suspicious about this man.

Monsieur Cornichon descended from his pulpit and was enthusiastically shaking Longfingers' hand when Cameron saw something glint very brightly as it passed from one man to the other.

There's something fishy going on over there, he thought.

'*Where* is that dreadful waitress?' cried Lulu, frustrated at the lack of service.

But Cameron continued to watch Erickson Longfingers as he made his sycophantic farewells to the fawning diners. And then, as if by magic, the man with the dandelion disappeared in the blink of an eye.

CHAPTER EIGHT

WAR

The bulky frame of Paloma Snuck hove into view. 'Cheese for two, please,' said Lulu abruptly, miffed at having had to wait so long.

'Very well, madame,' said Paloma haughtily, snatching the menu away and disappearing once again.

'I wonder how long she'll take this time,' Lulu said to Cameron – but almost immediately Paloma returned with a wooden cheese board and plonked it in the centre of the table.

'Cheese for two,' she announced. 'The cheese with the mould is a Tibetan Yak, the one with the herbs is fermented garlic, the yellow crusted one is a soured goat's cheese, and of course the strong-smelling mini cheese is Pico Stinko from Trans Mugrania. It has been matured underground for five years and holds a very *special* surprise.'

'Cool! I like surprises,' said Cameron, grabbing

the smelly cheese and popping it into his mouth.

'Manners, please, Cameron,' demanded Lulu. Paloma looked on with a wry smile. She decided it would be amusing to hang around to see the little brat's reaction to this gastronomic surprise.

Cameron was just about to have a good chew when he felt something wiggle about in his mouth.

'Eeeuugh,' he hollered, spitting the cheesy wiggle out of his mouth onto his plate.

Cameron and Lulu looked on in horror as they saw a green worm wriggling in front of their very eyes.

'Ah, you've found the surprise!' said Paloma with great relish.

'Why, you vile, NASTY little...' shouted Lulu. Picking up the green worm, she threw it at the smug assistant manager. It fell onto her ample bosom and wriggled its way down her cleavage.

'AAAAAAGGGGGGHHHHH!' screamed Paloma Snuck at the top of her voice, shaking her bosom from side to side and flaying her arms around, trying to get the worm out.

Just at that moment, three waiters came through the swinging kitchen doors, carrying enormous silver trays laden with food. Upon hearing Paloma's piercing scream, the waiters yelped and threw the trays high up into the air in fright. Up went the bloody bison steak, splash went the bloody meat juices, all over the spectacular glass chandelier. The ravioli of crocodile soared skywards until it landed – *SPLAT!* – on several rather astonished La-Di-Das.

'LOOK at me, look at me, DRIPPING in meat!' screamed a rather grand La-Di-Da lady with a bloody Bison steak perched on top of her head. Red and bloody juices from the steak streamed down her pale face and dripped onto her silver satin dress.

'COVERED! Covered in CROCODILE!' shrilled a La-Di-Da gentleman as he disgustedly wiped his white face of crocodile sauce and picked the crocodile ravioli out of his silk pocket.

Silence. Then a ripple of sniggers began to arise from the Hoity-Toitys. It passed from one person to another, all the time gaining momentum, increasing to an infectious giggle and slowly building into a wave of raucous laughter.

'How deliciously delightful,' said one. 'Those La-Di-Das covered in meat – that'll teach them.'

A thin white lady rose up in fury from her table. Her coiffured white hair was streaked with red meat juices and around her thin white neck hung meaty entrails, dangling like a string of meaty pearls. Her trout-pout lips, normally a pale salmon pink, were now the colour of blood. She scooped up fish eyes by the handful and hurled them furiously at a Hoity-Toity woman who was laughing like a hyena. *SPLOSH* went the sticky fish juice all over her face.

The fat-faced woman recoiled in horror as fish eyes stared back at her from the folds of her fur coat. Out went the airs and graces, gone were the genteel manners – it was time to get even!

'FISHING!' screamed the La-Di-Das, gathering their army.

A scaly gentleman picked out a slippery slime fish from a large water tank and marched over to an old Hoity-Toity opponent. He slapped his fat face with the fish, leaving the imprint of the tail on his ruddy cheek.

'Enough is enough!' bellowed a Hoity-Toity, thrusting her arm in the air. She threw her massive fur coat to the ground, picked up a roast rump of camel as if it were a rugby ball and ran towards a very old, sneering La-Di-Da lady. The wily old lady waited until the bellowing bison was very close, and then stuck out her silver-sequined foot. *CRASH*. The ruby-clad Hoity-Toity fell to the floor like a sack of potatoes.

'HUNTING!' bellowed the Hoity-Toitys, calling their group to arms.

A cowardly La-Di-Da man, who'd been hiding under a table, decided to make a quick get-away. 'Where do you think you're going!?' hollered a Hoity-Toity farmer at the top of his voice. He grabbed the longest spiced meaty entrails he could find, tied one end in a circle and threw it in the air.

SWOOSH! The entrail lasso wrapped itself around the coward's neck and the poor fellow fell abruptly.

'Food fight!' shouted a delighted Cameron.

Now it was a free-for-all. It was mealtime mayhem, culinary chaos, as dish after dish of meat or fish was thrown willy-nilly at the enemy.

Nobody was left untouched, not even the Pearl of Pimple.

A massive roast rump of camel fell onto her enormous wimple and crushed all the summer flowers. Her attendants scarpered off as her enormous hat collapsed. She was horrified. *I'll hide under the table,* she thought, crouching down – but not before a slimy fish flew through the air and slapped her in the face.

'Sniveller!' screamed the Pearl.

The Meddling Sniveller had also been hiding under a table, looking for a clean exit to the door. 'Ghastly people,' he muttered, forgetting his position as a spiritual advisor. 'It's now or never!' He gathered up his orange cassock and made a run for it. His little fat legs had almost made it to the cloakroom when a stodgy liquorice roly-poly pudding caught him in the face and knocked him out cold.

'Come on, Cameron, we're leaving,' announced Lulu, wiping the corners of her mouth with a napkin.

'Into the battle!' exclaimed Cameron, as he

wheeled himself out from behind the table.

They ducked and dived the continuing food fight as they picked their way through the battle zone towards the entrance.

A mortified Monsieur Cornichon had been running in and out of the fray. His black frock coat was covered in duck pond pudding. Curried fish guts stained his smart grey waistcoat.

Cameron and Lulu caught the back of him, running from the middle of the battleground. He was screaming at the top of his voice. 'Please... Please... stop zis nonsense! We are supposed to be civilised grown-ups... NOT little children!'

But to no avail. Everyone carried on chucking food, ignoring his appeals.

He turned around and leaned against the banister of his pulpit, just as Cameron and Lulu came towards him. 'You!' he spat angrily as he looked for someone to blame.

'A *good* afternoon to you, Monsieur,' said Lulu politely.

'Please *don't* send us the bill,' said Cameron.

Monsieur Cornichon glared at them angrily but had nothing to say. The nosh nightmare had taken a new turn. The Hoity-Toitys had upturned their tables and were building battlements while the La-Di-Das had picked up their chairs and were using them as shields.

'*Please* no! Zey are veeeery expenseeve,' screamed an exasperated Monsieur Grandee Cornichon, flaying his arms around in despair. Meanwhile Cameron and Lulu, as cool as cucumbers and amazingly unscathed from any flying food, exited the restaurant and ventured back out into what remained of the day.

CHAPTER NINE

THE ONLY WAY IS UP

'Let's go home and put our feet up. I'm gasping for a cup of tea,' said Lulu, as they strolled back through Gitwick Gardens. She was so relieved to be out of that bizarre restaurant. Then she remembered. 'Oh no!' she said. 'We still have to get up all those stairs.'

'The lift might be fixed,' said Cameron hopefully.

'Don't count on it,' said Lulu as she closed the gate to the gardens. 'Not with that lot in charge. I'm surprised *anything* gets done.'

Back at the bottom of Grimthorpe Towers, they found, to no great surprise, that the lift was still out of order 'until further notice'.

'Aaaaah!' Lulu screamed in frustration.

'Mum! Calm down. Count to ten,' said Cameron.

'Well, I suppose it's pointless getting my knickers in a twist over it. After all, nothing has been straightforward today. It'll have to be the stairs. Seventeen floors though!'

Cameron remembered the words of the singing scroll: *'Think hard about what you'll achieve, when helping others when in need.'*

The chair's the key, he thought. *It worked with the Elvis legs. I wonder… would it work again? It would be the best way of getting to the top.*

'Mum, what about the chair?' Cameron asked.

Lulu laughed affectionately. 'Were you thinking about dancing your way up the stairs?'

But Cameron was thinking of something a little different. Perhaps some magic to help him *and* his mum. What had been the trigger in Mr Poppet's shop? The singing scroll had sung: *'So make a wish, count ten to zero, believe in you and be the hero.'* He remembered that he had really *wanted* to dance. Was it the concentration alone?

Cameron closed his eyes and started to concentrate very hard. As he did so, the tiniest of spiders dropped down on its thread from the helmet above Cameron's head and dangled in front of his face. Cameron tried to brush it away.

'Seventeen floors up,' he chanted, as he tried to visualise some sort of contraption to get them to the top of the building. But each time he uttered the words, the spider swung back and tickled his face.

Flipping spider, he thought.

All of a sudden, the chair shuddered and shook. The antennae began whirring and flashing about his head... *BRR... BRR... BUZZ... BUZZ...* An intense light flashed and started to spin the chair around in a golden tornado. He felt his whole body being suspended in the air, supported by nothing but sheer energy. An incredible warm feeling completely enveloped him, and he began spinning around so fast that he became very dizzy. If he was honest, it was a little bit scary. He felt, for the second time, the strange melting feeling all around him. But this time he knew he wasn't standing in a pair of mechanical legs. What had he wished for? The intense light started to dim and ebb away. And then he heard his mum's voice.

'Blimey, Cameron, you have a powerful imagination!'

Cameron cautiously opened his eyes. He found himself looking at his mum through four bulbous spider's eyes, each reflecting a different image. Through one eye he saw Lulu's amazed expression; through another, a little dog barking. On either side he could see Grimthorpe Towers and the children's playground nearby. He was sitting in a pod-like cockpit, supported by eight hinged mechanical legs.

'Wow, a spider machine!' His eyes darted around the pod, which was similar in shape to the helmet above his chariot. He was sitting in his purple quilted seat but across his lap was a golden scroll-shaped panel with two buttons either side of a sphinx's head joystick.

'Dizzy!' said Cameron as he pushed the joystick to the right. He could feel the cockpit dip a little, the joints of its legs bending, before it straightened up again and scuttered to the right. 'Let's see what this thing can do!' Cameron rotated the joystick in a circular movement. The spider machine scuttled around in a fast-moving circle, its golden metal legs rattling and scratching against the concrete. He pushed the joystick to the left and the metal insect scuttered again to the front of the building. 'Awesome, I'm like Spider-Man! I could climb up the wall!'

Lulu stared at the strange-looking contraption. Its hard golden shell shone in the sunlight like an out-of-place Christmas bauble. The external sides of the cockpit were decorated with the wings of the sphinxes, which sat either side of the four thick-glass spider's eyes. The golden greaves, previously from the front of the chair, were now the front part of the spider's legs; the antennae rested on the top of the cockpit; and underneath the spider's eyes stared the face of a sphinx.

'Is there room in there for me?' asked Lulu. She was trying hard not to show her reluctance at Cameron having total control of this odd-looking contraption.

But Cameron wasn't listening. He was far too busy thinking about ascending the face of Grimthorpe Towers in his new spider machine. He looked down at the control button and saw the pink button flash.

Well, it's not flashing for nothing, he thought, and confidently slammed his hand down hard. A strong steel cable shot out from underneath the sphinx's face and sped through the air like an arrow.

Lulu and Cameron watched in amazement as it soared towards their balcony on the seventeenth floor, twirled and spun itself securely around the balcony railing. Metal on metal. *SHWACK!*

The spider machine jolted a little and pulled back as the cable attached itself. Cameron moved the joystick forward and the spider jerkily travelled forward across the concrete floor before beginning to climb up the face of the building.

'This is so cool! It's using the steel cable like a spider uses its thread,' said Cameron as the spider started its ascent.

'Please be careful!' shouted Lulu, who could hardly bear to watch.

CLINK... SCUT... CLINK... SCUT... CLINK... SCUT... the legs of the machine nimbly crawled up the wall in quick, agile movements, following the cable.

Cameron was concentrating very hard and becoming more confident by the second. The orange light flashed as he approached any open windows.

Uh oh! Better avoid them, thought Cameron, moving the joystick.

Down below, Lulu was worried. She wasn't used to her son being so active in this way. 'Be careful!' she yelled when the machine climbed another floor and 'Watch out!' when she thought the metallic spider was going to smash through a window.

As he reached the eighth floor, Cameron saw something that took him somewhat by surprise. Sitting in their front room were a middle-aged couple, watching the telly and having a cup of tea in nothing but their underwear!

'Have you seen the new-fangled window cleaning machine, Bert?' said the woman to her husband, pointing at the spider machine. Her bits and bottom bobbled and bounced as she calmly left her armchair and walked towards the window to get a better view.

Cameron couldn't help himself. It was so funny! He tried to suppress a chuckle but as the woman moved closer to the window, he started to get a serious attack of the giggles.

SCRAAAAAAAAA... the spider's metal legs scraped against the wall as they slid down the brickwork. Cameron was jolted in his seat. He'd have fallen into the back of the pod if it wasn't for the control panel across his waist holding him fast.

'What just happened?' he asked out loud, as he clutched the sides of the chair. He felt queasy.

Through the spider's top eye-window, the brickwork seemed to be sliding from left to right, left and then right again, as the pod swung on its steel cable from side to side. From the bottom window, all he could see was the undulating view of the ground beneath him.

'Oooh,' groaned Cameron. The swinging spider was making him feel *very* disorientated.

'Are you all right, Cameron?' shouted Lulu. She had noticed the antennae on top of the cockpit had stopped spinning. 'You need to stay *focused*!'

'Back in control, back in control – gotta get back in control,' muttered Cameron to himself. 'Don't worry, Mum!' he shouted. He screwed up his eyes and really concentrated on the task in hand. He heard the sound of the antennae buzzing again as he regained his focus. He thrust the joystick forward. The spider machine stopped swinging, its hinged mechanical legs connected with the wall, and it started to climb the brickwork once again.

Better! thought Cameron.

A seagull flew past. Cameron looked back, momentarily taking his hand off the joystick. The antennae stopped spinning and the spider machine started to slowly slide down the building again.

'Concentrate!' yelled Lulu.

Cameron made another quick recovery, determined to master his focus. But just when he *really* thought he'd got the hang of it, the little spider dropped straight in front of his face again.

'Go away!' yelled Cameron, and his concentration broken, he completely lost control.

The spider machine slowly slid down the face of the building. The pointed tips of its legs dragged along the brick work. Sparks flew as metal scraped against brick. There was an awful, grating *SCRAAA!* as the tips of the metallic spider's legs dug into the brickwork and left a trail of gouged marks down the building.

KER-THUMP, KER-THUMP, KER-THUMP! beat Cameron's heart. His dreams of being Spider-Man had been well and truly dashed!

The spider machine dropped a couple of metres in one sudden heart-in-mouth movement. Cameron needed to act fast but he had lost all his concentration. It was time to be back in his wheelchair. He looked down at the control panel and slammed the flashing pink light.

WHOOSH! There was the enormous golden flash again as he felt his body thrust into the air. Grimthorpe Towers disappeared and he felt that now familiar feeling of everything melting around him. He was falling backwards at super speed... falling... falling. All he could hear was the sound of his heart beat. All he could see were spinning golden lights. And then there was *silence.*

He opened his eyes. No more spider machine. No more spinning golden lights, only big silver bins and the smell of rubbish. He was sitting in his golden chair in the forecourt of Grimthorpe Towers with Lulu standing in front of him, looking concerned.

'Are you all right?' she said, giving him a hug.

Cameron was gobsmacked. He stared blankly for a few moments. 'It didn't work.'

'It did,' said Lulu, 'you just need to focus a little more.'

His mum was right. And Cameron knew it. Next time he wouldn't allow his thoughts to wander off. *Focus, focus, focus* would be his mantra.

'Oh well. Stairs, here we come,' said Lulu, making light of the task ahead. She grabbed the handles of Cameron's wheelchair and pushed him through the forecourt and entrance to Grimthorpe Towers.

Lulu heaved and pulled the wheelchair up the stairs with Cameron in it, step after step, floor after floor. *THUMP, THUMP, THUMP!* went the golden tyres against the concrete steps. Lulu panted and puffed, cursed and cried out. 'Talk about an uphill struggle,' she said to Cameron at one of their many breaks on a landing. Sweat poured down her face and neck. Her clothes were soaked and stuck uncomfortably to her skin and her back ached terribly. By the time they reached the seventeenth floor, she was close to exhaustion.

It hadn't been easy for Cameron either. He felt so helpless again. The upstairs journey had been more than uncomfortable, and he had been jolted and jerked from one step to another.

They unlocked their front door and made their way through the hallway into the sitting room, not saying a word. Lulu picked Cameron up out of his chair and they collapsed on the sofa together. Within minutes they were both fast asleep.

And while Cameron and Lulu slumbered, the little spider spun its web between the antennae on the top of the helmet on Cameron's magical chair.

– CHAPTER TEN –

UP AND AWAY

Cameron woke in his own bed. The last thing he remembered was collapsing on the sofa with Lulu. *Mum must have carried me into my room during the night*, he thought. Above his bed dangled the handle of his lifting pole, or his monkey pole as he called it. He pulled back the bedclothes, gripped the pole handle and swung his legs into the chair next to his bed. He checked the time on his alarm clock: 10.45 am. It was late morning and strangely quiet. Lulu was an early riser even if she'd had a late night. Normally Cameron was awoken to the sound of his mum's dreadful singing. This morning he couldn't hear a thing, let alone a bad note. Something wasn't quite right.

Better check on Mum, he thought as he wheeled his way down the hallway in his chair towards her bedroom. He popped his head around the door. Lulu heard it creak and opened her eyes.

'I feel absolutely appalling,' she croaked. Her face was pale and drawn. 'Think I caught a chill in yesterday's downpour. And my back is as sore as hell from all those stairs.'

'Oh, poor you! Can I get you anything?' sympathised Cameron.

'I'm all right for the moment,' said Lulu. 'I'll shout if I need something. Fix yourself some breakfast. You'll have to have your shower later.' She closed her eyes and turned over slowly in her bed.

'Fine by me!' Cameron replied. Showering was a lengthy process involving his mum, a special chair, pulleys and, worst of all, soap.

He made his way to the kitchen and sorted himself out some breakfast. He watched the telly while eating his cornflakes and played with the small plastic Roman chariot which had come free with the cereal packet. That is, until its wheel broke. He went back to his bedroom and tried to read but his mind was elsewhere. He returned to the sitting room, turned on the telly and watched cartoons for a bit but it was no good.

The thought of losing control of the spider machine yesterday really bugged him. It hadn't been as easy as the Elvis dancing machine. His mum had been right when she had reminded him to stay focused. He just hadn't managed to get the hang of it and had lost all control.

Bit rubbish really, he thought. The fact that his mum was ill in bed only made him feel worse.

An enormous seagull flew past the sitting room window and landed on the balcony railing.

'So you're back,' said Cameron, convinced it was the same seagull from yesterday, the one that had made him lose his concentration.

'*SCWAAH!*' squawked the seagull, looking at Cameron intently before catching a hot air current and flying off.

If only I could do that, thought Cameron, as he watched the seagull glide away, staying aloft without a single beat of its wings.

He looked down at his chair, imagining how it would look when transformed into a magnificent flying machine. Being able to fly in the sky like a bird... Now that would be *something else*. People would look up and think he was a superhero soaring through the sky. None of the boys at school had a flying machine – he would be the first. That would trump their skateboards!

But what would Lulu have to say about it? She would be so mad at him for making a transformation without her there to supervise.

I could just wish for a quickie: to fly around for ten minutes and then fly back. Mum wouldn't even know! I won't lie to her... she just won't find out.

Cameron wheeled himself from the sitting room to his mum's bedroom and popped his head around the door again. She was snoring gently.

'Out for the count. Good!'

He made his way back to the sitting room and opened the balcony door. *Focus... focus...* he thought to himself. He stared at the blue sky and the billowy white clouds for a few minutes before he closed his eyes and concentrated.

He thought of the sphinxes' wings on his chair. 'I want my chair to fly like a bird,' he said to himself over and over, imagining a flying chariot fit for Apollo, the Roman god of the sun. 'A *magnificent* golden flying chariot.' He began to count. 'Ten... Nine... Eight... Seven... Six... Five... Four... Three... Two... One... Zero!'

The chair shuddered and shook. The antennae began whirring and flashing about his head... *BRR... BRR... BUZZ... BUZZ...* The intense light flashed and started to spin the chair around in a golden tornado. Once again he felt his whole body held in the air, supported by nothing but sheer energy. The incredible warm feeling completely enveloped him and he began spinning around at super speed. The strange melting feeling was there again but this time he felt a lot less scared. He felt his whole body being suspended in the air. He opened his eyes.

'WHOAH!' he shouted. He was suspended in mid-air. Directly beneath him, and just beyond the balcony, hovered a flying machine. *SWISH!* A force of energy sucked him down and dumped him into the quilted purple seat. *SLAM!* The control panel slammed down over his lap, like a safety bar. He was sitting in a magnificent flying machine! The sphinxes' heads were either side of his seat, their golden wings unfurled, and on top of the right-hand sphinx was the joystick. It started to dawn on Cameron how powerful his imagination could be.

The sudden drop of his body into the flying machine caused it to rock to-and-fro like a carriage on a Ferris wheel. Butterflies fluttered in his stomach. He gripped the sides of the machine. A purple light flashed on the control panel. Without really thinking, he slammed his hand down on it. The rocking movement stopped.

'Phew, at last!' Cameron looked down over the side of his seat, taking stock. It was exhilarating and terrifying all at the same time. 'Focus, focus...' he said to himself, trying to steady his nerves.

He placed his hand on the joystick, pulling it backwards by mistake, just a little bit... The flying machine jolted dramatically and reversed, crashing the tip of one of the broad sphinx wings into the window pane. *CRASH!* The glass shattered onto the floor of the sitting room. 'Whoops!' The orange button on his control panel was flashing madly but Cameron ignored it. 'Gotta focus,' he muttered, pushing the joystick in front of him.

The flying machine lurched forward. Cameron could hear the antennae on the helmet whirring. 'Focus! I don't want anything to go wrong.'

The wings lifted, caught the air current and glided gently in the direction of Potwell Park.

Lulu sat bolt upright in her bed. She thought she had heard smashing glass. Had she dreamt it? Or was it the telly? The apartment was *very* quiet. No sounds of Cameron. She couldn't hear him playing. Perhaps he was reading? But where on earth had the sound of smashing glass come from? She put on her dressing gown and slippers and went into his bedroom. No Cameron. She checked the bathroom and the kitchen – he wasn't there either. She ran into the sitting room to find the carpet covered in glass!

'Leave him for five minutes and look what happens!' She tiptoed acrobatically amongst the broken glass before rushing out through the balcony door, only to see her son in the distance, flying unsteadily in a golden winged machine.

'Cameron, you… you… you come back here right now!'

She hurriedly got dressed and, grabbing her keys,

ran down the corridor and leapt down the stairs two at a time.

Cameron could hear the gentle swish of the wind as it blew through the wings' golden feathers. He flew cautiously at first, concentrating on where he wanted to fly and how fast he wanted to go. He could hear the machine's humming sound as he flew above Potwell Park. He turned the joystick sharply to the left and the machine quickly banked according to his instruction.

'I'm getting the hang of this. Now let's try something a little more daring.'

He looked up. The clouds above looked ever so near. What if? He concentrated on flying the machine towards the clouds and pulled the joystick right back. The machine climbed quickly. Cameron's adrenaline kicked in as he flew higher and higher. Soon he was amidst the wispy white cloud and within seconds he was surrounded by white, just cold white. 'Brrr!' The drop in temperature was immediate. His teeth started to chatter. 'Cold, too cold.'

He gently pushed the joystick forward and slowly pierced the cloud again to emerge into the blue.

He looked over the side. He was just passing over Pimple High Street and could see the busy crowds in the street.

I wonder if they can see me? he thought to himself.

He passed over Gitwick Gardens and could see the Epicuriousity Café, dazzling in the bright sunshine. An enormous purple and green striped marquee had been erected nearby and a large crowd of people were gathered outside.

Looks like the circus, he thought to himself. *I wonder what's going on?*

Curiosity got the better of him, and pushing his joystick forward, he began his descent.

CHAPTER ELEVEN

THE GARDEN PARTY

In the large purple and green marquee, the final touches were being made for The Twenty-Seventh Gitwick Garden's Annual Soiree for the Illuminating Society of La-Di-Das and the Bedazzling Association of Hoity-Toitys. Relations between the two groups had been very frosty after their unexpected food fight the day before. The Pearl of Pimple, as leader of the Assembly, had rallied the two opposing groups and asked them (nicely) to *forget* about the previous day and to *focus* on the garden party. Trauma therapists, councillors and the occasional plastic surgeon had been called in to soothe nerves, massage egos and heal the wounds of the food fight. VIPs and dignitaries were coming from all over the country and the La-Di-Das and Hoity-Toitys needed to impress. It was going to be a very special occasion.

The assembled crowd were wearing their finest jewels, medals, tiaras and gold watches, all to be auctioned in order to raise funds for the Pimple Tornado appeal. The money raised would go to help those most in need and to repair the storm damage. The famous auctioneers Smotherbys had been asked to evaluate all the valuables and oversee proceedings.

The gardens soon filled up with hundreds of people sipping wine and enjoying the unusual food supplied by the kitchens of the Epicuriousity Café. Champagne corks popped against a background of heavenly harp music. It was imperative that both groups should remain amicable and be able to sit side by side once again in order to mark this momentous occasion.

But things were far from resolved. Beneath the gaiety and laughter, the chinking of glasses and the veneer of good manners, lay bloodcurdling hatred.

As the women exchanged air kisses, the Hoity-Toity ladies leaned towards their adversaries' cheeks and whispered, 'Lovely to see you,' through clenched teeth.

'Yes, lovely to see more of you… *again*,' replied the La-Di-Da ladies as they wetly shook their adversaries' hands.

The Hoity-Toity gentlemen thumped their opponents' backs in mock joviality, knocking the wind out of them. 'Oh, there you are. We finally hunted you down.'

And the La-Di-Da gentlemen spluttered over their foes with rank, fishy breath.

This charged atmosphere, thinly disguised with insincere smiles and two-faced tittle-tattle, filled the gardens. The harpist, keen to bring a little heaven to the hellish surroundings, plucked his angelic strings so eagerly that he cut his finger. A drop of blood dribbled down one of the harp strings.

The women had all tried to outdo each other, their lofty hats piled high with all manner of stuffed birds, ribbons, silks and jewels. The gentlemen's waistcoats hung with gem-encrusted gold watches, their pockets stuffed with money to win, or to lose, at a game of cards. Emeralds hung from earlobes, diamonds rested on heaving bosoms, and on every finger and toe rested rubies and sapphires as large as rocks.

Paloma Snuck was uncomfortable in her best green-silk dress. It hadn't *always* been so small. The fact that she had overheard two of the staff comparing her to a stuffed cabbage did not make her feel any better. She was running around barking orders at waiters, and keeping out of Monsieur Cornichon's way. He blamed her for allowing 'zat dreadful Mother and 'er son' into *his* exclusive restaurant. She kept a watchful view of him from the corner of her eye as he strode around the gardens, a clipboard and pen in one hand, nervously crossing off items on his To Do list. She had never seen him so jumpy.

A flash of gold in the sky suddenly caught her attention. *That's odd*, she thought. It looked like some sort of flying machine. But it was rather too small to be a plane and its wings flapped like a bird. It immediately disappeared into the clouds and she soon forgot all about it. There were other, *far* more important things to think about.

She turned her head and caught Erickson Longfingers making his way out of the marquee and tying up the looping before instructing two security guards to stand guard. He lent down and picked a fresh dandelion from the grass and placed it in his buttonhole. *Strange choice of flower for a buttonhole*, she thought. He looked ill at ease as he made his way towards Monsieur Cornichon, who was making small talk with the Pearl of Pimple.

'Mr Longfingers, how delightful that you are here again to amuse and entertain our little clan. I hear that you have a fantastic new act. I am *soooooooooo* looking forward to it,' gushed the Pearl of Pimple.

'Yes, your Pearliness, you are all in for a *big* surprise and you will only have to wait a few more minutes,' said Longfingers, bowing his head and smiling slyly.

'Delightful, delightful. And how amusing and capricious of you to wear a common weed in your jacket,' said the Pearl, gliding her finger over his buttonhole.

'*Adieu, adieu,* kind lady,' said Monsieur Cornichon, wiggling his fingers at her as she turned and re-joined her guests.

'Are you all set?' Longfingers asked Cornichon nervously.

'Yes, I am ready and have instructed ze staff to stand on zer guard outside ze tent when I give ze orders,' whispered Cornichon.

'That's good. On no account must they let anyone in. There must be no disturbances.'

'We must be quick when we do what we 'ave to do,' said Cornichon.

'That's right. And be calm. Once they're under, I'll be on hand to help you. And remember... whatever you do, don't look at it!'

'Ok, ok. Are you sure zey will not remember?'

'Listen, mate, by the time I've finished with them, they won't even remember who they are,' said Longfingers, suddenly dropping his affected accent for the far rougher, harsher genuine article.

Paloma Snuck continued to watch the two men from a distance. They seemed to be having an intense conversation. Perhaps Mr Longfingers was nervous about his new act? He was normally much more relaxed. What on earth were the two of them up to?

Monsieur Cornichon caught Paloma's eye and beckoned her to him.

'Miss Snuck, send your staff into ze gardens and

bring ze guests into the marquee. Mr Longfingers is ready to start 'iz performance.'

'Oh happily, Monsieur Cornichon, happily,' gushed Paloma. Now it was time to for *her* to crack the whip, something she always looked forward to. She exited determinedly, only to be called back by her boss again.

'I must 'ave your word zat on no account are you or any of ze staff to look into the marquee during ze performance.'

'No sneaky peek-a-boos,' said Mr Longfingers, exaggerating the expression as if Miss Snuck was a toddler.

'And no flirting wiz ze curtain,' added Monsieur Cornichon.

'No snooping through the looping, Ms Snuck,' re-joined Longfingers, miming someone popping their head through a curtain.

'As you wish, gentlemen,' said Paloma, somewhat baffled. She waddled off to bark their instructions to the staff.

Hundreds of guests made their way into the marquee, curious to experience the afternoon's entertainment. Inside, the excitement grew. The animated crowd whispered to each other in anticipation as Monsieur Cornichon and Mr Longfingers arranged the guests and their chairs around a centre stage.

Monsieur Cornichon stepped up. He tested the microphone, checked his cuff links and raised his arms.

'Monsieurs *et* Mesdames, I have ze pleasure of introducing to you ze entertainment for ze afternoon, our dear friend Erickson Longfingers.'

Longfingers made his entrance from one of the marquee side flaps, proceeding down the aisle to enthusiastic applause. He had replaced his usual straw boater with an enormous purple turban and around his shoulders he wore a cloak of emerald green satin. Longfingers stood on the stage and bowed. He lifted his cloak and fifty pastel-coloured budgerigars flew out, nesting in some of the hats of the ladies sitting in the front row, much to everyone's amusement.

'Bravo, bravo!' shouted the ecstatic crowd.

Erickson Longfingers stood triumphantly on the stage, his arms outstretched, revelling as the applause washed over him. His beady eyes darted around the room, searching for his accomplice, Monsieur Cornichon. He spotted him at the back of the tent and winked at him knowingly. Cornichon winked back in return, then pulled out a trolley on which was placed an extraordinary-looking object. The crowd's attention followed Monsieur Cornichon as he wheeled the mysterious object towards the centre stage.

The object in question was large and tear-shaped, two metres high and one metre wide. It was encased in coral and ivory and decorated with gold filigree. Coiled around it was a black ebony dragon inlaid with silver. The guests gasped at its beauty, whispering to each other, 'What on earth could it be?'

'Monsieur Cornichon, would you do me the honour of being my assistant and turning the key?' asked Longfingers. The audience tittered politely. One Hoity-Toity guffawed loudly. The *idea* of Monsieur Grandee Cornichon being an assistant in any capacity was highly amusing.

'Certainly, my *dear* friend,' said Cornichon as he turned a large key at the base of the strange object.

The encasing slowly divided into four petals, opening like a mechanical flower. A melancholic music box tune filled the marquee.

'Oooh!' gasped the audience as the open petals revealed an opaque glass tear, a holographic clock embedded within it, its digits visible from every viewpoint in the large marquee.

'Your Pearliness,' announced Longfingers, 'my lords, ladies and gentlemen, for my next trick, I humbly beseech you to remain perfectly still and completely quiet as I perform an act of great wonderment and awe. What you see in front of you is no ordinary clock, and *time*, as you know, is of the essence.'

The clock emitted a strange humming sound and psychedelic colours spiralled around inside the glass tear. The holographic clock hands gathered speed as they raced around and around and a holographic pendulum swung heavily from side to side, filling the marquee with a mesmerising *tick-tock, tick-tock*.

'Ladies and gentlemen, I ask you to please focus on the clock and remember… *time is the only thing we can't afford to lose.'*

Longfingers repeated these last words over and over, in a soothing, hypnotic mantra. The guests stared fixedly in a catatonic gaze at the speeding hands and the swinging pendulum as the psychedelic colours radiated out from the clock and enveloped them in soporific stupor. They were so transfixed that they did not notice that Longfingers had stealthily made his way down from the stage and was now amongst them with his accomplice, Cornichon, divesting each and every one of them of their valuables. Every neck was relieved of a diamond necklace, every ear unburdened of an emerald earring, every manicured hand lightened of a ruby ring and every waistcoat and wallet cleansed of every pound and penny. The only sound to be heard throughout the great marquee was the ominous ticking of the clock and Longfingers' words over and over again: '*Time is the only thing we can't afford to lose….'*

CHAPTER TWELVE

CAMERON DESCENDS

PALOMA

Paloma Snuck put her ear to the side of the tent. There was complete silence apart from the loud *tick-tock* of a clock and Erikson Longfingers' voice repeating the same phrase over and over: '*Time is the only thing we can't afford to lose...*'

'Just a little peek-a-boo,' she muttered to herself, opening up the marquee looping to peep through. Immediately she could see what appeared to be an enormous clock placed in the centre of the marquee. The clock's hands whirled around frenetically as hypnotic colours pulsated from its face. All the guests stared at the clock like zombies, eyes wide as saucers. Erikson Longfingers and Monsieur Cornichon dashed in between them. They seemed to be caressing the guests' necks and ears and fondling their fingers. Even the auctioneers from Smotherbys were standing as still as goal posts. Something wasn't right.

'What are those two up to?' Paloma examined the crowd, looking for an explanation, but her attention kept being drawn back to the strange tear-shaped clock. Something compelled her to look at it. The hypnotic colours washed over her, bathing her mind in pink, yellow, purple and green until she too was transfixed. Soon all she could hear was the nonstop tick-tock, tick-tock of the clock and the hypnotic voice in her head telling her, *Time is the only thing we can't afford to lose...*

Lulu
Lulu had been running, running as if her life depended on it. She had lost sight of her son flying above her, and she was now more worried than she had ever been before. The last she had seen of him he had been flying towards Gitwick Gardens. After that, he had disappeared. She ran down Pimple High Street and across the road towards the entrance leading to Gitwick Gardens. Arriving at the grand iron gates, she immediately noticed not only that the 'P' in private had been restored to its correct place, but that there was a huge padlock and chain securing the two gates.

'Aaarggh!' she shouted, rattling the chain in frustration.

I'm going to have to climb the gate, she thought. But it wasn't that easy to climb. Its ornate bars with their sharp-pointed tips dug into her legs and feet as she hurriedly scrambled up. She managed to get to the top without impaling herself and was just swinging herself over when she was spotted by a policeman on his beat.

That's all I need, thought Lulu.

'Good afternoon, madame. Now… what, may I ask, are you doin' up there?' inquired the policeman.

'It's my son!'

'What about your son?' said the policeman, patiently waiting for an explanation.

'I've lost him! Or at least, the last I saw of him he was flying towards Gitwick Gardens.'

'Flying, you say?'

'Yes, flying!'

'So how old is your son?'

'He's nine.'

'And when exactly did your nine-year-old son get his pilot's licence?' said the policeman, taking out his notepad. *The boys back at the station are gonna love this!* he thought.

'Actually, officer, you're never going to believe this… he flew out of the window in his wheelchair. I know, I know, it's rather a tall story but this wheelchair is somewhat special.'

The policeman hesitated. This woman was clearly two sandwiches short of a picnic. Then again, a missing boy was something to be taken seriously.

'Madame,' he said eventually, 'I think you need to come down to the station with me.'

'I'm sorry, officer, I don't really have time to explain.' Lulu suddenly caught a glimpse of the flying machine, just as it nosedived through the clouds. 'Sorry, sorry, but I just have to go!' She leapt off the other side of the gate and raced off along the tree-lined pathway. All she could hear as she sped away were the angry curses of the policeman and the ripping sound of his trousers as he tried to clamber over the gate after her.

CAMERON

Things weren't going well for Cameron. The flying machine had dipped underneath the higher air currents and as a result the air stream wasn't as strong. He was beginning to lose his confidence. An enormous seagull wheeled in front of him.

'Seriously, are you following me!?' exclaimed Cameron. As soon as he said it, he regretted it. The flying machine was incredibly sensitive to any change in his thought. The whirring antennae above his head suddenly stopped and the flying machine's gentle hum went silent.

'Focus, *focus*...' he said to himself. But what he was feeling was panic. All he could hear was KERCHUNK, KERCHUNK, KERCHUNK as the chair spluttered to a halt. The feathered wings stopped beating and the machine briefly glided on an air current – before dramatically nosediving at an incredible speed, straight toward the occupied marquee.

The flying machine hit the marquee at full speed. Instinctively Cameron covered his face. *PING-PING-PING* went the rubber loops as it crashed through the flaps. A side pole that helped support part of the massive canvas structure was hit with such force that it buckled, causing part of the tent's roof to deflate. The massive span of the feathered wings knocked the guests and their chairs over and up as the flying machine hurtled through, causing a pile-up of people and furniture. It crashed into the centre stage and rebounded sharply, the chair spinning around in erratic circles until it finally came to a halt. Cameron slowly opened his fingers and peeped between them. What had he done?

CHAPTER THIRTEEN

REVELATION

Looking around, Cameron saw no clowns, no trapeze artists, no trumpeting elephants. Instead he saw dazed people lying on the floor, groaning or scrambling over each other. He recognised them as the horrible people that had been so rude to him and his mother at the restaurant the day before. Miraculously no one seemed hurt.

Amidst the chaos, Monsieur Cornichon was scrabbling around on the floor, trying to locate his bag of stolen loot. The clock lay in pieces beside him, its sinister spell now broken. All around him, confused and befuddled people were slowly coming to their senses.

'Yesterday ze food fight! Today 'avoc and chaos! I need to get out of 'ere,' Monsieur Cornichon announced, panic-stricken. He anxiously looked around but couldn't see Longfingers anywhere – or either of the bags of loot. He wrapped his cape around himself furtively and made a quick getaway.

As he came to, the last thing Erikson Longfingers remembered was shouting instructions to the seated mob. And then *CRASH!* Confusion. He was lying on the floor, dazed and disorientated. To make matters worse, a rather rotund Hoity-Toity gentleman was lying on top of him, moaning. He managed with difficulty to push the man off him, stood up and brushed himself off.

Events had taken an unexpected dramatic turn and he wanted to get to the bottom of it. *What* had happened? *Where* was Cornichon? His brain felt extremely muddled but it quickly regained some order as he remembered the most important thing – the loot! His eyes quickly scanned the room for its whereabouts.

And then he saw him. The *brat from yesterday.* What was *he* doing here? And what on earth was that extraordinary looking machine with enormous wings?

Cameron didn't recognise Longfingers immediately. The day before, he'd been wearing a stripy blazer and straw boater – not a green cloak. But as he turned around, Cameron recognised him immediately. Their eyes locked.

At this point, Lulu breathlessly made her entrance. 'Oh my stars, what's happened here!?' she gasped at the turmoil before her. But her immediate concern was for her son. She rushed as quickly as she could between the groaning Hoity-Toitys and the La-Di-Das, towards Cameron, and gave him a huge hug.

'You silly, silly, boy,' she whispered. 'Are you hurt?' She checked him over for bruises or any signs of damage.

'I'm fine, Mum. I'm *so* sorry,' said Cameron, giving his mum a big hug back.

'Thank God you are all right,' said Lulu, extremely relieved.

The Hoity-Toitys and the La-Di-Das were starting to come round. The mesmerising clock lay in pieces on the floor and with it, the broken spell. They moaned and groaned as they picked their bashed and bruised bodies up from the floor, mystified as to why they were sprawled there in the first place. As they became more conscious, they noticed the winged flying machine in their midst with Cameron still sitting in it.

'What beast is this!?' exclaimed a shrilling La-Di-Da, who had lost her glasses in the fray.

'Shoot it!' bellowed a befuddled Hoity-Toity.

'Cameron, *concentrate*,' implored Lulu. 'You need to get that thing back to its normal shape right now. We'll talk about your behaviour when we get home.'

Cameron closed his eyes tightly and focused on transforming his flying machine back into his wheelchair. He pressed the pink button and FLASH! An intense golden light filled the marquee, and everything started to spin around him. He was suspended in mid-air again, with that strange sensation of everything melting. WHOOSH! He was falling backwards at super speed... falling... falling. Then everything was still again.

'Oh no! Not *more* magic,' bellowed a Hoity-Toity, as the golden light filled the marquee.

'*Time is the only thing...* Oh! I've forgotten the rest of it,' said a confused La-Di-Da. In the flashing light and confusion, she thought she was still watching the hypnotic clock.

Amongst the pile of people, the mountain of chairs and the muddle and mayhem, Erikson Longfingers had now managed to retrieve *both* bags of loot. He was about to confront the brat and its mother when the mighty golden flash occurred. Longfingers couldn't believe it. One minute the brat had been sitting in a flying machine, the next in a golden wheelchair. If there was one thing he knew when he saw it, it was magic!

Time to go! thought Longfingers. He moved swiftly to the exit but tripped over the sprawled legs of a prone La-Di-Da. A sparkling tiara fell out of one of the black bags. He quickly picked it up, hoping that no one had seen it... but not before he had caught Cameron's eye.

He's got everyone's jewels! thought Cameron, putting two and two together.

Longfingers stared back at Cameron. Hatefully. Chillingly. And then he turned and scarpered, hiding the two bags of jewels underneath his green cloak.

The Pearl lay on the floor, crumpled and dishevelled. She didn't look like the Jewel of Pimple now. She flayed her arms around as she cleared the broken headdress from her face. She staggered to her feet. She'd broken the heel off her shoe and her beautiful, beautiful dress was ruined. 'My frock, my frock,' she whimpered. She suddenly noticed that her ring of office, an enormous emerald, was missing. She patted her head. No tiara either! She pulled at her earlobes. And no diamond earrings!

'Aaaaagghh!' she screamed. '*HELP!* My jewels, my jewels, they're all *gone!*' She threw a hand up to her forehead and affected a faint, pitching to the side, expecting the Assembly to gather around and catch her.

But while her scream brought everyone abruptly to their senses, it only sent the Hoity-Toitys and La-Di-Das looking for their *own* missing diamonds and rubies, sapphires and opals. The women frenziedly shook their hair in the hope that a tiara might fall out. The gentlemen rummaged hurriedly through their pockets in the hope of finding some loose change. Moaning, they crawled along the ground, desperately prospecting every square metre for a mislaid ring or a misplaced necklace. But to no avail. They found nothing. Nil. Zilch.

At that moment, the policeman rushed in, puffing and panting. While climbing over the gate, he had witnessed the strange flying machine torpedo into the side of the marquee but all he could see around him now were anxious, dishevelled people crawling about on the floor. Nobody seemed hurt. But why were they acting so strangely?

'Is everyone all right?' he enquired. 'Any broken bones?'

The crowd simply redoubled their wailing. One of them clutched at the policeman's ankles and he stepped back in surprise. That was when he spotted Lulu.

'Madam, don't think I've forgotten about you,' he said, pointing a finger at her.

The Very Meddling Sniveller stepped forward and held his hand up. 'Policeman of Pimple, a terrible act has been committed. These genteel people came here today to sell their precious jewels in aid of the worthiest of causes. I myself was auctioning the sweetest pair of emerald-encrusted cufflinks, given to me by my dear grandpapa. Now we have been robbed of every ruby, diamond and emerald. Officer, we have been fleeced of our fortunes, in broad daylight and these are the perpetrators.' He pointed an accusing finger at Cameron and Lulu.

'Officer, arrest these two scoundrels immediately!' screamed the Pearl of Pimple.

'Hang on a minute!' yelled Lulu. 'The officer caught me only a few minutes ago, climbing over the Gitwick Garden gate. How could I have stolen your jewellery? That's nonsense!'

'Must be the boy then. Arrest him!' yelled back one of the Hoity-Toitys.

'Lock him up!' shouted a large nosed La-Di-Da.

'Trespasser!' shrieked one Hoity-Toity.

'But I was only climbing over to fetch my son,' replied Lulu.

But no one could hear her. Everyone started to shout out his or her version of events. The besieged policeman struggled valiantly as he tried to quiet the hysterical crowd.

'Please, please, one at a time. I'll be interviewing you all individually so for the time being hold yer horses!' He turned to address Lulu. 'Madame, I'm going to have to ask you and your son to come with me for questioning.'

No sooner had the policemen spoken than the angry crowd encircled Lulu and Cameron, shouting and bellowing, hungry for justice. The noise was deafening. Some of the crowd grabbed hold of

Cameron's wheelchair and shook it as if they thought their jewels might fall out. Cameron had had enough.

'Shut up!' he screamed at the top of his voice. And to his surprise, they did. He supposed they weren't used to being spoken to in this way. Most of the time they would be giving the orders, not taking them. 'Thank you!' he said. 'For your information, the person who has stolen all your jewels and money is the man who wears the dandelion.'

'Erikson Longfingers? Surely not, boy! He is a dear, dear friend of ours!' replied the Meddling Sniveller incredulously.

'Well, I'm telling you, I saw him leave the tent with two large bags full of all your jewellery!'

'Impossible!' protested one Hoity-Toity.

'Unbelievable!' said another La-Di-Da.

'I know what I saw!' said Cameron defiantly.

'And that's why you and your mother are coming down to the station with me,' said the policeman firmly.

'Come on, Cameron, let's do what he says,' said Lulu.

The policeman was just escorting them through the angry crowd when Paloma Snuck burst into what remained of the tent, her hair tangled and knotted, her dress torn and covered in mud. With a crazed look in her eyes, she frantically ran around, shouting at the top of her voice to the jewel–less crowd. *'Time is the only thing we can't afford to lose!'*

– CHAPTER FOURTEEN –

THE DARK LAKE

Things weren't going well for Cameron and Lulu down at the police station. The atmosphere was so fraught you could have cut it with a knife. The air control office had reported a sighting of a strange golden aircraft flying unsteadily above Pimple. As Cameron had since transformed the flying machine back into his chair, Lulu denied there had ever been a flying machine in the first place. She didn't want to get her son into trouble. And Cameron certainly didn't want to tell the police that his chair was magic. That would lead to all sorts of complications.

But right now, the policeman was more concerned with the missing jewellery. He knew Lulu couldn't have been responsible – he had watched her climb over the gate at the time of the crime. (She was, however, lucky he wasn't going to press charges for her trespassing on private property.) He didn't think Cameron was the culprit either. He was only nine years old . But he clearly knew something. Especially about Erikson Longfingers and Monsieur Cornichon.

Cameron was *more* than happy to spill the beans about what he had seen. He spiced up the story by telling the policeman about the appalling food and the dreadful service in the restaurant the day before. Together with the statements from the Hoity-Toitys and the La-Di-Das, the policeman gradually put the pieces of the puzzle together.

After a few hours of interrogation, Cameron and his mother were released with a warning, delivered in very strong words, about unlicensed flying machines. It was dusk as the exhausted pair made their way home.

'This magical chair has turned from a dream-come-true into a nightmare,' said Lulu.

A dream-come-true into a nightmare… Cameron cringed when she said it. She was right. The only transformation that had gone to plan was the mechanical legs. He had been so happy to dance like Elvis. It had all gone downhill after that. The spider machine had been a flipping disaster, and then he'd immediately topped it by torpedoing a flying machine into a tent. What if he'd hurt someone? Perhaps magic was like driving or voting: you had to be old enough.

I wish Mr Pea was about, he thought. *He'd be able sort me out.* But he didn't even have his mobile number or his email address. *How am I going to get hold of him?*

They made their way through Potwell Park. The clear-up operation following the tornado was well underway. Fallen branches had been stacked in neat piles, and huge mounds of debris, blown in from all over Pimple, were waiting to be removed.

Old ornate gaslights lined the central path. A pale moon hung in a blue-black night sky, casting an eerie light onto the water in the lake.

'Look, there's a little Mini. There, in the water!' exclaimed Lulu. 'Let's take a look.'

'Hmmm,' muttered Cameron. He was still thinking about how to contact Mr Pea and whether to give his chair back but he followed Lulu as she diverted from the path towards the lakeside.

The little car's glassy headlights peeped out from underneath the water like two doleful eyes. The car was hooked onto a wire rope that was attached to a winch on the back of an odd-looking vehicle parked at the side of the lake.

Continuing their walk, they passed a thick clump of bushes near the water's edge. Cameron turned his head, hearing the sound of sleepy ducks. And then he saw it glistening. The light of the moon caught the brilliant, sharp cut of diamonds in the grass.

'Wow, Mum! Look at this!' exclaimed Cameron, pointing excitedly at his find.

Lulu walked over towards where it lay. She bent down and picked it up. It was an exquisite necklace: twenty mine-cut diamonds on a single thread with a fringe of pear and oval diamonds dangling underneath. She had never held such a beautiful piece of jewellery.

'How absolutely *stunning*,' purred Lulu, bewitched by the sparkling stones. 'It must be part of the stolen hoard the police are looking for.'

In the nearby bushes, slumbering a few metres away, was Erikson Longfingers. Having escaped with his stolen treasure, he had thought it best to lay low for a while. The private grounds of Gitwick Gardens were crawling with police looking for him. His plan was to wait until dark and then escape to a hideaway in downtown Pimple so he'd decided to get forty winks, hidden in the bushes with the two bags of jewellery still slung around his neck for safekeeping.

Drowsily he heard two people talking. Blinking away sleep, he parted the branches of the shrubbery with his long fingers to get a better look. He could just about make out a hand holding a diamond necklace. He recognised it immediately. It was the star piece, one of the finest in his newly acquired collection. Now fully awake, he sprung out from the shrubbery like a jack-in-the-box and made a grab for the necklace.

'You're the mother of that nosy brat,' he spat, recognising Lulu in an instant.

'Oi,' shouted Cameron in defiance, but sitting in his chair, he could do nothing.

'Give that back to me,' yelled Longfingers as he took another swipe at the necklace, losing his balance and knocking Lulu to the ground.

'Get off me you, you—' Lulu gasped, winded from Longfingers' attack.

Longfingers grappled with Lulu, trying to prise her fingers open to seize the diamond necklace. But she held on to it firmly, gathered all her strength and pushed him off. Struggling to her feet, she faced her attacker with her back to the lake.

Longfingers leapt up and lunged at her again. The weight of the two bags slung around his shoulders gave him extra impetus, and he flew forward, slipping on the muddy banks of the lake. Instinctively he grabbed hold of Lulu to regain his balance, but in doing so, he dragged her with him into the water. There was an almighty splash as the two bodies crashed into the muddy lake.

Lulu was terrified. She was *in* the water – her biggest fear!

'I can't swim!' she screamed, dropping the diamond necklace as she scrambled to keep her head above water. *Someone to hold onto, someone to hold onto* was her only thought. She reached out in panic and clasped her hands tightly around Longfingers' neck. Longfingers grabbed hold of her hands and forcibly prised them apart but Lulu tightened her arms around his waist in an effort to save herself.

'Please somebody help!' screamed Cameron, beside himself with worry. He felt so helpless, just sitting there, not being able to do anything!

Longfingers dragged his feet through the heavy mud towards the deeper water. *The stupid woman can't swim. I'll flaming drown her!* he thought darkly, pulling the clutching, dead weight of Lulu with him.

Lulu clung to Longfingers for dear life. Her stomach and lungs were now taking in so much water that she kept coughing and retching. 'There's nothing... nothing... underneath me!' She felt the horrible man's hand on her head as he tried to push her under the water.

'HELP! Somebody, please... HELP my mum!'

Lulu could hear Cameron's muffled plea from underneath the water. A hundred images flashed through her mind – her son's cheeky smile, the magical wheelchair, Cameron dancing like Elvis, the spider machine. Despite the pressure on her head, she pushed upwards with all her might, burst to the surface and gasped loudly as she took a breath. She had to breathe. She had to live.

'Under you go,' shouted Longfingers, as he pushed her head under again. He could hear the brat's voice screaming for help in the distance. Lulu flayed her arms around in desperation but he knew she would weaken. Soon her hands went slack. At last, he was rid of her. Now to escape before anyone responded to the brat screaming on the bank. Longfingers struck out for the far shore of the lake as Lulu's weak body sank lower into the inky depths.

The lake was wider than Erikson Longfingers anticipated and the fight with Lulu had sapped his energy. The heavy bags tied around his neck were saturated and heavy, *really* heavy. He kept dipping below the waterline as the weight of the bags dragged him down. As hard as he tried, he couldn't keep himself afloat. He kept being pulled down, only to fight his way back up again, splashing, spluttering and cursing. Eventually, shattered and spent, he realised that the only way he was going to save himself was by abandoning his precious cargo. He untied both bags from around his neck and reluctantly let them go. He watched in despair as his treasure sank further into the murky depths. He couldn't bear it and reached out to grab them again… But his long fingers grasped at nothing. It was too late. With his lungs full of water, he swam back up to the surface, coughing and spluttering. He could see on the distant shore, the outline of Cameron's wheelchair with the gas light flickering overhead. He struck out for the opposite side of the lake and crawled onto the muddy bank.

'Gone, all gone. All my lovely jewels!' he howled.

Cameron's ears momentarily pricked up, hearing Longfingers' desperate scream, but right now all he could think about was his mum.

It had all happened so quickly. In the gathering darkness, he'd just about been able to see the shadowy shape of his mum, flaying her arms around and screaming for help. And then – nothing. Was she dead? Where was she? He felt so helpless.

The only thing he could think of was the chair's magic. 'Come on, come on,' he said to himself, hot tears running down his cheeks. 'You've got to do it this time. I'll never ask for anything else again, I promise. I'll give the chair back. Just make this work, one more time. Please, Mr Pea, please help me!'

He closed his eyes and focused one more time. 'A boat to save my mum, a boat to save my mum,' he repeated over and over again. He pictured a coracle, a small round, lightweight boat even older than the Romans. But the more he wished and tried to focus, the more nothing happened. No whirring antennae. No golden tornado. No spinning around. No boat. *Nothing.* The magic simply wasn't working.

Suspended in the water, drifting slowly downwards, Lulu was at peace. Around her, all noise had ceased. A last thought floated into her mind. It was of Cameron.

'*Mummmmm!*'

Cameron's scream, from the depths of his soul, pierced through the water, through the translucent surface, through the dark, into Lulu's consciousness.

Her mind focused as she snapped to. Sheer determination and the image of her son drove her as she clawed her way back to the surface. Closer and closer. She burst above the waterline. With huge, forced gasps, she drew air into her tortured lungs, desperate for breath.

Cameron's sobbing instantly stopped when he saw the dim shape of his mum re-emerge at the water's surface. He breathed out loudly in relief. He could hear again the desperate splashing of arms. 'Mum's *still* alive, she's still *ALIVE!*' He rubbed the stinging tears from his eyes. His adrenaline kicked in as his eyes darted around the scene in front of him. His mum had come back but she still couldn't swim. He had to find the answer. He had to save his mum. The submerged Mini's luminous eyes stared balefully at him. 'That's it,' he cried. 'Grab the wire rope, Mum! Grab the rope!'

Lulu could just make out the rope attached to the Mini. She mustered every available ounce of energy and, thrashing her arms around, she grabbed the rope for dear life. Lifting one foot onto the submerged car's bonnet, she clambered on to the roof, exhausted.

Tears of relief streamed down Cameron's face. His mum was safe.

An engine suddenly started up and a faint smell of toffee and pineapple filled the air. The winch on the back of the truck whirred as it started to turn the wire rope. Moving forward into the pool of gaslight, the truck slowly pulled the Mini out of the water. As the vehicle came into view, Cameron immediately recognised the pink and sky blue paintwork with its green trim.

'It's Mr Pea, it's Mr Pea,' shouted Cameron. And he wheeled himself frantically towards the Intergalactic Dream Factory.

Within minutes, the waterlogged Mini was out of the water, with Lulu lying safely on top. Cameron heard the engine stop. The door flew open as Mr Pea jumped out and shot over to where Lulu lay. He gathered her body up in his strong arms and carried her over towards Cameron, placing her gently on the ground at his feet.

'One mum, safely delivered,' said Mr Pea. He gently swept her bedraggled hair away from her eyes and moved her onto her side. 'Thank goodness I got here in time.'

Lulu retched onto the ground. She turned her head a little. She could see the man above her: the silver beads in his hair, glowing against his skin, his kind concerned face with eyes shining green, so very green. And then she saw Cameron. Her boy... her child.

'Thank you... *thank you,*' she whispered and then closed her eyes, exhausted.

Cameron lent over in his chair and placed his hands on her shoulders. The touch of her child's hand was like an electric current. She struggled to her feet and wrapped her arms around her son.

'Thank goodness you're alive, Mum,' Cameron whispered. They hugged each other fiercely.

'Now, first things first, let's think about getting you and your mum home,' said Mr Pea. He wrapped a warm blanket around Lulu's shoulders before escorting her towards the Intergalactic Dream Factory. Cameron followed in his wheelchair.

'Are you Mr Pea?' murmured Lulu.

'That's right, lady. Now hush yourself and rest.'

'How come you were here?' said Cameron.

'I'm never far away,' Mr Pea said with chuckle.

'It didn't work, *again*!' Cameron said mournfully. 'The chair, it didn't work... the *transformation* didn't work.'

Mr Pea lent down towards Cameron. His green eyes shining. He tapped him on the forehead with his finger and quietly rapped.

> *'Life is hard and sometimes tragic,*
> *The answer sometimes lies in magic.*

Today you've done extraordinary 'ting,
Saved your mum when she can't swim.
Tomorrow there's a trail to find,
Prepare and focus in your mind.
No emotion, no distraction,
If you want the magic action!'

CHAPTER FIFTEEN

A PLAN

A hotchpotch of colours, smells and lights swirled around Cameron's head. Mr Pea's green eyes beamed as brightly as traffic lights. He chuckled. 'Welcome to the world of the magical highway!' Cameron saw, or thought he saw, trails of sparkling lights. Neon-pink signposts indicating routes to the milky way, all jumbled up with the smell of chocolate and strawberries from the purple exhaust fumes.

Cameron awoke. He turned his head and checked his alarm clock. 8.33 am. He was in his bed at home. *Weird*, he thought. All he recalled was getting into the Intergalactic Dream Factory with Mum and Mr Pea and the dream he'd just woken up from. Everything else was a blank. And then he remembered. His mum had nearly *drowned!* His heart skipped a beat at the thought of it.

He could just make out two voices whispering in the hallway. A man and a woman. What on earth was going on? The woman's voice was definitely not his mum's. He heard the front door open and shut. 'Goodbye,' said the man. 'I'll pop back later.'

Cameron pulled back his bedclothes, gripped his monkey pole and swung his legs into his wheelchair. His chair seemed to have an extra sparkle about it this morning. The sphinxes seemed more polished, the wheel spokes gleamed and the tyres definitely had more bounce. *Had Mr Pea given it an MOT?*

He wheeled himself over to his bedroom door, opened it and popped his head out to have a look. The woman's voice was now coming from his mum's bedroom. *Who is she? Why is she here?* He made his way down the hallway and knocked on his mum's bedroom door.

'Come in,' said the voice.

'Ruby, it's you! What are you doing here?' said Cameron as he opened the door.

The panniers of Ruby's skirt seemed to fill the room. Her hair was messier than usual and her face was only half made-up.

Still bonkers was Cameron's first thought.

'Your mother phoned me earlier this morning, asking me to come and help. Well, well, what an *extraordinary* looking chair.' She clapped her hands together in delight. 'Ooooh, *sphinxes!*'

Cameron smiled but now was not the time to talk about his chair. He wanted to see his mum.

Lulu was propped up in bed with lots of pillows. Her face was pasty white, perspiration glistened on her forehead. With one hand Ruby wiped Lulu's brow with a flannel and with the other she gave her a sip of water.

'Mum, how are you? How are you feeling?' said Cameron anxiously. He reached out to hold her hand.

'The doctor's just been. I didn't get over the chill the other day and nearly drowning just made it worse. I just need some rest,' croaked Lulu. 'Ruby's going to look after you, so be a good boy, please? For Mum?'

'Of course, Mum. Anything.'

She squeezed his hand. 'Just one thing. How on earth did we get home? I don't remember a thing.'

'I don't know. I can't remember much either. I was hoping you could tell me.'

But Lulu had already drifted off.

Inky ran down a cascading curl from Ruby's mountain of white hair and sniffed the air inquisitively. Poe popped his little head out of her corseted bodice to see what was going on.

'Let's leave her to sleep,' said Ruby quietly as they made their way into the living room.

Throughout the day, between playing games on his computer, Cameron popped along to check on his mum. She was exhausted and slept for most of the day. The trauma of nearly drowning had been too much for her.

It was four o'clock in the afternoon when Ruby appeared with a tin of fantasy-in-vanilla cupcakes, proudly announcing to Cameron, 'A new batch from yesterday. I'll pop the kettle on and we'll have a feast. I wonder if your mum would like one?'

Oh no, not more fantasy-in-horribles. YUK! thought Cameron as she piled the cupcakes onto a plate in the kitchen. 'Not sure if she's up for cake,' he called quickly to Ruby.

'Oh well, more for you then. I'll just go check on her,' said Ruby, placing the plate next to Cameron. 'Eat up!'

Cameron quickly looked over the sitting room. Where to hide them? He wheeled himself over to the sofa and unzipped one of the cushions. Grabbing five of the cakes from the plate, he stuffed them inside and zipped it back up again. He gave the cushion a massive thump to plump it up and threw it back on the sofa.

Phew... just in time, he thought as Ruby re-entered the sitting room.

'My, my, what a hungry little chap you are,' said Ruby, counting the cupcakes. 'Five of them in under five minutes... *very* impressive. You must really like them!'

Ruby's supper was even worse than her cupcakes. She boiled the peas for over an hour!

Euugh, thought Cameron as she ladled the green goo onto the plate, next to burnt fish fingers and soggy, greasy chips.

His mum's words rang in his head. 'Always be polite to people... *if* possible.' While eating a particularly burnt fish finger, he wondered if this could be considered a *not* possible occasion. But he was too well brought up to say anything horrid. Besides, he was thinking about his chair.

'Penny for your thoughts,' said Ruby. Cameron seemed miles away. She moved his plate of half-eaten food to one side and sat next to him. 'Why don't you tell me about the chair?'

Could he tell her? It was different to when he was in the police station. Ruby was a friend and a neighbour. She had helped him out when the lift was broken. Yes, he decided, he could confide in her. He trusted her.

'The chair is magic,' he said, looking her straight in the eye.

'I *knew* it!' exclaimed Ruby, clapping her hands enthusiastically. 'That explains the sphinxes. They represent power and strength, truth and secrets, mysteries and riddles – all the *ingredients* of magic. And how did you come by this magical chair?'

'Mr Pea gave it to me.'

'Mr Pea?'

At this point, Cameron decided to spill the beans... all of them. He spoke so quickly and excitedly that Ruby had trouble keeping up. He told her about Mr Pea and his Intergalactic Dream Factory appearing at the end of a rainbow. He told her about the singing scroll, about the tale of the chair's first transformation into a dancing machine – he even treated her to a verse of 'Jailhouse Rock'. He re-lived the terror he had felt clambering up the wall in the shaky spider machine so convincingly that Ruby poured herself a big glass of wine to calm her nerves. By the time he'd recounted the story of the flying machine crashing into the marquee, Cameron thought Ruby's eyes were going to pop out. And the story of Erikson Longfingers trying to drown Lulu and swimming away with the stolen jewels left Ruby shocked and horrified.

'That *dreadful* Longfingers,' said Ruby indignantly. 'Your poor mother! And stealing all those jewels! Someone should do something. You know, take action, get on his trail, make things right.'

That's when Cameron remembered and repeated the rap to Ruby:

'Tomorrow there's a trail to find,
Prepare and focus in your mind.
No emotion, no distraction,
If you want the magic action.'

'That's what Mr Pea told me last night,' Cameron finished.

'Interesting... interesting,' said Ruby. She was deep in thought as she turned her large diamond ring round and round her finger. Cameron could see that it wasn't real. It looked very different to the ones he'd seen at the Epicuriousity Café. It glittered brightly as it caught the light... *reminding* him.

'That's it, the jewels!' he exclaimed.

'The jewels?' asked Ruby 'What do you mean?'

'That's how we make it right!'

'Is that what Mr Pea meant?' asked Ruby.

'The trail, yes, that's it, it's a treasure trail. That *must* be what he meant.'

'Do you know where they are?'

'Longfingers had them when he fell in the water... they were wrapped around his neck. I saw them,' said Cameron ardently.

'Perhaps he dropped them in the struggle?' said Ruby. 'They might be in the lake We have to find them!'

Cameron's heart sank. If the jewels *were* in the lake, how was he going to get them back? His swimming had improved since going to the disability swimming club but he couldn't swim that far. He doubted if Ruby could do it either, especially in that *silly* dress.

'*Esprit, mon ami. Esprit!*' said Ruby. She rose from her chair, straightened her back and thrust her chin forward. 'Would Napoleon have achieved so much without *esprit*? Do you think the great General Julius Caesar would have conquered Gaul without *esprit*?'

Cameron's mood lightened. Ruby knew about Julius Caesar. Impressive.

'Would Hannibal have marched from Spain to Italy if he had been despondent? *NON. Mon ami, NON!*' said Ruby. She lifted her right leg onto her chair at the final '*NON!*'

Blimey, she's getting carried away, thought Cameron.

'Mount Everest was climbed with bravery, fortitude and stamina,' said Ruby dramatically, climbing onto the chair.

Cameron winced. *I hope she doesn't fall off.*

'We shall conquer the waves of the great lake, like the invincible Admiral Nelson on the high seas,' shouted Ruby, climbing from the chair to the table and thrusting her right arm triumphantly in the air.

Absolutely bonkers, thought Cameron. But he was impressed nonetheless.

Ruby looked down at Cameron. He was grinning. She climbed off the table, onto the chair and then back onto the floor. She brushed her dress down and patted the mountain of white hair.

'Besides, you're lucky... you've a *magical* chair,' she said as if it was the most usual thing in the world.

Cameron was convinced. Ruby was an inspiration and his mind was made up. He *was* a lucky boy. He was going to use his magical chair to find the jewels!

'Let's do it,' said Cameron, with new determination.

'That's the spirit!'

And so, on a summer's evening, on the seventeenth floor of Grimthorpe Towers, Cameron and Ruby hatched their plan for retrieving the stolen jewels.

CHAPTER SIXTEEN

UNDER THE MOON

Cameron and Ruby stood in front of the gates of Potwell Park. It was three minutes past ten o'clock. The ornate gaslights on the path ahead stood strong and silent, their yellow light flickering against a dark night sky. Cameron pushed the gates open. The dramatic incidents of the other night came flooding back. A sliver of silver light shone from the crescent moon.

'Oh, the white goddess,' sighed Ruby.

But Cameron didn't hear her. Bright torchlight suddenly flashed across their faces, blinding them both.

'Cameron Tiberius McPherson?' The voice was familiar. Cameron could see the silhouette of a policeman's helmet.

'Uh oh,' muttered Cameron under his breath.

'You seem to be making a habit of entering parks without your mother!'

'Hello, officer,' answered Cameron, half-heartedly.

'And who might you be?' inquired the policeman, smirking as he flashed his torchlight over Ruby's crinoline dress. *This'll be good*, he thought to himself, eagerly waiting to hear what Ruby had to say. *Can't wait to tell the boys down the station.*

'I'm Ruby Broomhead, officer,' cooed Ruby, fluttering her false eyelashes.

'Rather late to be walking around parks, isn't it?' said the policeman, staring at Ruby's mountain of white hair. Inky and Poe popped their twitching noses out to see what was going on. *Blimey!* thought the policeman. *This just gets better.*

'We're... ah... researching a project,' Cameron shot back quickly.

'Yes, a project,' echoed Ruby.

'It's for my Roman summer holiday project.'

'Yes, Roman project,' Ruby repeated, winking at Cameron.

'And it's got to be done at night!' said Cameron.

'*Yes*, at night!' said Ruby. She fluttered her fingers in the air in the hope of distracting the policeman. His bewildered gaze followed them. 'It's all about...' She suddenly caught sight of the moon again. 'Diana... the Roman goddess of the moon.'

'Bit of a tall story, don't you think?' said the policeman, unimpressed.

'The moon only comes out at night,' Ruby declared as if she was the only one who knew this fact.

'Only at night, eh? Well I *never* knew that!' said the policeman drily.

'Are we breaking the law?' inquired Ruby sweetly.

'Err... no, but...'

'Then we'll be on our way. A *very* good night to you, officer.' Turning away from the policeman with a theatrical flourish, Ruby called out into the night, 'Oh, Diana, goddess of the moon, where are you?' And with that, she marched off purposefully in the direction of the lake.

'Night, officer,' said Cameron, smiling.

'The moon makes you mad, you know,' retorted the policeman as he turned to leave.

'Yeah, yeah, she *loves* the moon,' replied Cameron, moving to follow Ruby in the direction of the lake.

The memory of last night's drama had heightened Cameron's senses. Every noise seemed to be louder – the wind blowing through the treetops, the creaking boughs, the rustling leaves. The sudden hooting of an owl made him jump. He could just make out the flapping shadows of birds as they flew from tree to tree. Leaves crackled under the chair's tyres as he wheeled himself towards the lakeside.

'Stand close and hold my hand,' said Cameron. There needed to be room for Ruby in this transformation. He needed a friend by his side.

'Right here,' said Ruby grabbing hold of his hand.

Cameron remembered the words from the singing scroll:

> 'Think hard about what you'll achieve,
> In helping others when in need.
> So make your wish, count ten to zero,
> Believe in yourself and be the HERO!'

He squeezed Ruby's hand and closed his eyes, thinking, focusing, visualising with all his might. '*A submarine to find the lost treasure... a submarine for Ruby and me.*' He counted in his head. *Ten... Nine... Eight... Seven... Six... Five... Four... Three... Two... One... Zero!*

Suddenly the chair shuddered and shook. The antennae began whirring and flashing about his head... *BRR... BRR... BUZZ... BUZZ... FLASH.* The chair spun around in a golden tornado. *WHOOSH!* He felt his whole body being suspended in the air, supported by nothing but sheer energy. An incredible warm feeling completely enveloped him as he spun around faster and faster. Cameron felt, for the fourth time, the strange melting feeling all around him. The flash had appeared brighter this time, the lights more dazzling, the magic more intense. *SPLASH*. The sudden impact of the submarine hitting the water jolted him. He opened his eyes and looked around.

He was sitting in the pressure bubble of a submarine. It was similar in shape to the golden chair's helmet and was not unlike the cockpit from the spider machine. It had a water-screen that was transparent and curved. It was like looking out of a large glass bowl. As the half-submerged submarine bobbed up and down in the water, Cameron could see the trees through the top of the water-screen and the water in the lake through the bottom.

'Wow!' said Cameron, looking around the pressure bubble. 'It worked.'

'All in one piece,' said Ruby, adjusting her hooped skirt. It wasn't the most practical thing to wear in a small submarine so she pulled up the crinoline and pushed it behind her, over the back of her seat. Cameron could see her long knickers underneath. 'That's better,' she said, making herself comfortable.

Cameron wanted to giggle but knew he had to focus on the control panel in front of him. All he had to do now was figure out how to pilot the submarine.

In the centre of the panel was a directional joystick with multicoloured buttons either side.

So far so good, thought Cameron. *Just like before.*

To the far left and right of the joystick there were two handles embedded in the panel. Cameron gripped them and squeezed them gently. They were soft and flexible underneath.

'I wonder what these do?'

Above and to the right was an oxygen gauge, not unlike a temperature gauge, with red and green indicators on either side. The central arrow was currently pointing to green.

'Hmmm, now for the headlights,' muttered Cameron to himself. A button flashed yellow and Cameron pressed it down firmly. Powerful beams of light shone from the eyes of the sphinxes either side of the transparent pressure bubble, piercing the gloom of the lake's dark depths. At last Cameron could see the exterior of the submarine in front of him. The pressure bubble in which he and Ruby sat was placed on two golden tanks shaped like sphinxes' wings, which thrust forward in front of the water-screen.

'Let there be light!' exclaimed Ruby.

'Right, now we are getting somewhere,' said Cameron. The blue light flashed. Cameron pushed it down. *SCHLOOP!* The golden ballast tanks sucked in water and the submarine began to submerge. 'Now, let's get that treasure,' said Cameron. He moved the joystick to the left and the submarine responded accordingly.

Mr Pea's words rang through his head. *'No emotion, no distraction.'*

'Focus, focus...' muttered Cameron to himself. He thrust the joystick forward and the submarine surged ahead.

CHAPTER SEVENTEEN

RECOVERY

The underwater world was very different to anything Cameron had experienced before. Large rocks covered in green algae and moss lay at the bottom. Dark green plants swayed to and fro in the water's strong undercurrents. A large pike suddenly shot out of an abandoned supermarket trolley before shooting back in again. It was an eerie world, fascinating and alien.

'Over there!' pointed Ruby excitedly. The lights from the sphinxes' eyes caught the shape of what appeared to be large black sacks. The submarine glided gracefully towards the mysterious bags lying at the bottom of the lake and hovered just above them.

Inky popped his head from Ruby's bosom to see what was going on.

'They're not the treasure bags,' said Cameron. 'I wonder what they are?' A purple light flashed.

Cameron pressed it down and two pincers shot out from the bottom of the submarine.

Cameron looked down at the control panel. He needed to find out how to operate the pincers. 'I wonder what the red button does?' Without waiting for it to flash, he pressed it.

SWOOSH! Bubbles of water billowed out of the ballast tanks and the submarine started to ascend.

'Ooops... don't want to do *that*,' said Cameron. The blue light flashed again. Cameron remembered. Blue was the colour to descend. He pressed the blue button. *SCHLOOP!* The ballast tanks sucked in the water again and the submarine submerged.

'We have to find out what's in those bags,' said Ruby.

'I think I know what to do,' said Cameron. Just as he said it, the two handles flashed green. Cameron grabbed them and squeezed. The golden pincers snapped open and shut. They worked just like a fairground candy grabber.

Squeezing the handles again and twisting them from side to side, Cameron manoeuvred the pincers over the black plastic bags and tried to pick them up.

'Yes!' he shouted in glee as the pincers successfully grabbed hold of the bags. But in pulling the bags back up towards the submarine, the pincers tore into the plastic, spilling their contents all over the bed of the lake.

'It's just old bottles and rubbish,' said Cameron. He squeezed a handle and the left pincer picked up one of the fallen bottles. The label read, 'The Epicuriosity Café'.

'Isn't that the restaurant you told me about?' inquired Ruby.

'Yes, the one with the rubbish people,' replied Cameron.

'Rubbish people who dump their rubbish in a lake. Disgraceful,' sighed Ruby indignantly. 'Come on, let's keep going.'

As they continued their journey, Ruby and Cameron saw rubbish scattered everywhere. Cameron operated the golden pincers to sort through the debris but there was still no sign of the jewels.

'*Mon cher*, I fear we will never find this treasure,' said Ruby, stroking Inky's head. The two mice had settled down now and were lying in her lap. 'Strange…' she remarked. 'These two are normally so active.'

Cameron checked the gauge on the control panel. The little arrow now pointed towards red.

'Uh oh, I think we're running short of oxygen.'

'Oh dear. I hope my little squeaks are going to be all right.' Ruby was starting to get alarmed.

'I think we have about thirty minutes left,' said Cameron. 'We need to get a move on!'

Ruby continued to stroke her little mice. 'Come on, my dears, stay with us!'

'The bags have to be here somewhere... they *have* to be,' said Cameron determinedly. A thought occurred to him. 'Ruby, can you take control for a while? There's something I need to do.'

'OK,' said Ruby grabbing hold of the joystick. 'But hurry!'

Cameron closed his eyes. He tried to visualise the bright glittering jewels lying at the bottom of the lake. His head swirled with past images. The Pearl's glittering necklace. The gold medals on the gentlemen's lapels. He thought of the Hoity-Toity's ruby tiaras and the La-Di-Da's emerald rings.

'I can't seem to control the submarine. It's turning around of its own accord.' Ruby sounded very flustered.

'Don't worry,' said Cameron, 'let the submarine take us to the treasure.'

Ruby let go of the joystick as the submarine gracefully spun a half circle and glided forward in the opposite direction. The powerful beams from the sphinxes' eyes scanned the bottom of the lake in all directions, casting bright white light into the dark. A beam caught something in the crevice of a large rock that lay ahead and a flare of red flashed back.

Cameron and Ruby gasped with excitement. Could this be the treasure?

'I think we've found something!' Cameron exclaimed.

'I do hope so. I'm beginning to feel a little drowsy.'

Cameron manoeuvred the submarine until it was in front of the rock. The purple light flashed again. He pushed the button and the right-hand pincer shot through the water, straight into the crevice. As soon as the right handle flashed green, Cameron gripped it firmly and squeezed twice to open and shut the pincer. He pulled the handle up to bring it back. The pincer emerged, revealing a stunning necklace with glistening fiery red rubies.

'Oooohh!' cooed Ruby.

'The rest of the treasure has got to be around here somewhere!'

The headlights criss-crossed the lake bed in front of them. A light flashed from the gloom.

'Over there!'

The headlights homed in and a burst of dazzling light blinded them both.

'There, there!' exclaimed Ruby, pointing excitedly.

Cameron guided the submarine closer. Perched on top of a pair of rusting oil drums were two black bags, tied together with a piece of rope. Peeping out of the top of one of the bags was a brilliant tiara with its diamonds sparkling in the headlights. Erickson Longfingers' loot!

The green handles flashed again. Cameron squeezed and the left pincer grabbed the two bags of treasure and brought them back to the submarine.

'We did it, Ruby, we did it!'

In that moment, that one moment, Cameron realised that he had focused successfully. Without any emotions or distractions. Exactly as Mr Pea had said. He had found the treasure. He had learnt how to control the magic!

Ruby tapped the oxygen gauge. The arrow was pointing dangerously to the right side of red.

'Time to go home,' she breathed hoarsely.

Cameron pressed the red button. *SWOOSH!* Bubbles of water pushed out of the ballast tanks and the submarine started to ascend to the top of the lake. Bubbles... bubbles... bubbles...

Then air flooded into the pressure chamber as they breached the surface. The central arrow on the oxygen gauge bounced back to green. Cameron and Ruby gasped in relief as they refilled their lungs with clear, sweet air. Ruby looked down at her lap to see Inky and Poe perkily chasing each other's tails.

Cameron steered the submarine towards the cluster of bushes by the lakeside. Looking at the bank, he gave Ruby a nod and grabbed her hand. 'Magic time,' he said. He closed his eyes and thought about sitting back in his chair.

FLASH! A golden ball of light spun around and around, filling the submarine with its intense glow. Suspended in mid-air, he felt that strange sensation once more, of everything melting around him. *WHOOSH!* He started to fall backwards... falling... falling... falling. He heard the sound of wind in the rushes. He opened his eyes. He was sitting back in his chair on the banks of the lake with two bags of heavy wet treasure on his lap and Ruby was standing next to him, Inky and Poe now revived and back in her hair.

'That beats my parachute jumps!' said Ruby, lifting her crinoline up to air her knickers.

'Yeah, it was kinda fun, wasn't it? The best yet!' replied Cameron with a smile. 'Now we just have to get these jewels back without anyone getting any ideas.' He glanced warily into the dark around them. 'That Erikson Longfingers could be anywhere.'

'We could hide them?' Ruby suggested.

'How?'

'Underneath my dress, of course,' said Ruby. She turned around and rummaged around in her petticoats. 'Necessity is the mother of invention,' she announced, brandishing a belt made from her stockings and suspenders. She picked up the two bags of jewels and tied them to it. She lifted her dress up, secured the belt around her waist and smoothed her skirt back down again.

'Behold, the wonders of the crinoline!'

They headed back towards the path. The yellow light of the gaslights was comforting after the dark depths of the lake. The closer they got to Grimthorpe Towers, the more they realised how exhausted they were. Exhausted but over the moon. They had found the jewels at the bottom of the lake. They could now return them to their owners. The auction for the tornado appeal could finally go ahead.

Back in his bed, long after Ruby had tucked him up and said goodnight, Cameron tossed and turned in his sleep. He was having a dream... a dark dream... about Erikson Longfingers and Monsieur Grandee Cornichon.

— CHAPTER EIGHTEEN —

TWO BOILED EGGS

Erikson Longfingers was sitting at the kitchen table in a flat. The flat was a dark, damp and dingy basement with very little light and no comfort to be found. It was situated off a horrible, rat-infested alleyway in downtown Pimple. In front of Longfingers were two boiled eggs with stale toast soldiers standing by. Longfingers sipped tea from a dirty chipped mug. The front door slammed. He jerked his mug and spilled hot tea all over his lap.

'Aaagghh!' screamed Longfingers.

'Aaagghh!' screamed Cornichon.

Longfingers and Cornichon had both been living on top of each other for days. Neither had been able to return to their respective homes while the police were still on the hunt for them.

Monsieur Cornichon had returned after popping out to get some provisions with the few pennies they had managed to scrape together. Scared of being recognised, he had disguised himself with a different toupee.

'Damn it!' he announced. 'Zey had no croissant. How am I expected to start the day wiz out my French pastries!'

The local shops could only be described as grotty. The heady days with the Hoity-Toitys and La-Di-Das at the Epicuriousity Café seemed a long time ago.

'You bleedin' frightened the life out of me!' spat Longfingers. 'Look what you made me do!' He scrambled around for something to wipe the tea off his trousers.

'Oh *do* stop your whinging! Zat's all you've done for days,' said Cornichon, pulling the toupee off his head and throwing it on the kitchen table.

Longfingers picked it up and wiped the tea stain off his trousers with it.

'Don't use this as a dish cloth. 'Ave you no respect?' said Cornichon, pulling the tea-soaked toupee from Longfingers' hands. He put the shopping bag down and took out a copy of the local newspaper, *The Pimple Post*, from the top of the bag. 'Look! We've made ze front page!'

'The front page!' said Longfingers enthusiastically, grabbing the newspaper out of Cornichon's hands.

'It's nothing to be proud of, you idiot!' snapped Cornichon.

Longfingers studied the newspaper. Underneath the headline – 'BOY FINDS TREASURE' – was a photo of Cameron, Ruby and Lulu.

He started to read the article out loud, his voice becoming more and more outraged as he read on.

'A nine-year-old boy, Cameron Tiberius McPherson, and his neighbour, Ruby Broomhead, were helping police with their enquiries this week in connection to the stolen jewels of Pimple. The jewels, stolen from the Assembly's annual summer party, were to be auctioned in aid of The Pimple Tornado Appeal. Cameron McPherson claims to have found the missing jewels in bushes near the lake in Potwell Park. According to the police report, Cameron and his mother, Mrs Lulu Saint-Mildred-Tudor-Mole-Flouncy-Bibbitt-McPherson, encountered the jewel thief, Mr Erikson Longfingers, a self-styled magician, the previous night. The police would like any information regarding the connection of Erikson Longfingers and his accomplice, Monsieur Grandee Cornichon, the former manager of the Epicuriousity Café.

'A spokesperson for the Hoity-Toitys and the La-Di-Das confirmed that the leader of the Assembly, the Pearl of Pimple, will be rewarding Cameron McPherson with a free fairground day for all the children of Pimple.'

'Bushes!? BUSHES!?' snapped Longfingers. 'I didn't leave them in the bushes! I dropped them at the bottom of the lake. They got the facts wrong!'

'And now it's too late to go back and get zem. You fool,' hissed Cornichon.

'Oh, suddenly it's *my* fault! None of this would 'ave happened if you'd stuck by me instead of running off at the garden party, you... you... French coward! We should be out of the country by now, sunbathing on a beach sipping cocktails. Instead we have no money, no jewels. *Nothing.*' He was making so much noise that the neighbour above started banging the floor. Longfingers and Cornichon looked up at the ceiling and froze. The last thing they needed now was attention from the neighbours.

'That little blighter...' whispered Longfingers. 'That sow of a mother... I could...' He picked up a teaspoon and smashed the two boiled eggs until there was nothing left but a yellow yolky mess.

'*Pull yourself together,*' hissed Cornichon, 'Zere are more important things to do than to wallow in self-pity. We have to forget about ze jewels for ze time being and focus on what to do next.'

'What's more important than jewels and money?' said Longfingers. He looked around the basement with its spiders' webs and dirty walls, its smelly drains and broken windows. It wasn't the five-star hotel he had imagined. He banged his head repeatedly on the table and started to cry like a baby.

Cornichon looked down at *The Pimple Post*. That idiotic boy's face smiled back at him. He leant in closer, studying the picture. There was something especially odd about that wheelchair. He noticed the sphinxes on the side of the chair and remembered he had seen them on something else. But what? He thought back to the fateful afternoon of the hypnotic clock and it slowly dawned on him... He grabbed the lapels of Longfingers' jacket.

'Listen to me. Zat boy crashed into the marquee in something that flew. From what I remember, it looked similar to the wheelchair that he's sitting in here.' He jabbed at the newspaper. 'It's no ordinary chair. Look at it – it could be made of gold! If we can only get our hands on it...'

The events of the last few days had thrown Longfingers off course but now he was beginning to remember. Cornichon had at least been good for something. He had jogged his memory. Longfingers thought back to the hypnotic clock. With his own eyes he had seen the boy crashing into the marquee in a flying machine; had watched as it transformed into a wheelchair. It was one of the most powerful acts of magic he had ever seen. He grabbed the newspaper and stared at the picture of Cameron. Cornichon was right. The wings of the sphinxes on the wheelchair looked remarkably like the wings of the flying machine. What sort of chair was it? What secret powers did it hold? If nothing else, it flew!

'It's *magic* alright,' said Longfingers 'It's a transforming magical chair. I saw it with my own eyes!'

'We need to get hold of it and get rid of ze boy,' said Cornichon, stroking his chin. 'Just imagine, if it can transform into anything, what other powers does it hold?'

'That must have been how he got the treasure. But how did he know the jewels were at the bottom of the lake? He must 'ave X-ray vision or something. And how does a nine-year-old brat get hold of a magical chair in the first place?'

'Zat will probably remain a mystery unless we get 'old of it,' said Cornichon.

'So how are we going to catch the little blighter?'

Cornichon picked up *The Pimple Post* and re-read the newspaper article for himself. It didn't mention where the boy and his mother lived or what school he went to. But then he saw the clue.

'Ze Pearl of Pimple is rewarding Cameron with a free fairground day for all ze little brats in Pimple. Zat's it! All ze information we need to know. Ze fair is opening on Monday. Zat gives us a few days.'

'But how do we get in?'

Cornichon grabbed the tea-stained toupee lying on the kitchen table.

'I 'ave an idea.'

He leaned over and whispered into Longfingers' ear, just in case the neighbour upstairs was listening.

CHAPTER NINETEEN

ALL THE FUN OF THE FAIR

'Welcome dear, *dear* Cameron. Pimple's little hero,' gushed the Pearl of Pimple as she rushed towards him. She was walking so quickly that the attendants holding the poles that propped up her enormous headdress had trouble keeping up.

Blimey, let me get out of the car first! thought Cameron as he wheeled himself down the little ramp from the stretch limo. The Pearl stood in front of the limousine's door with a stretched smile and open arms.

Please, please don't hug me, thought Cameron.

But he remembered his mum's golden rule of politeness and smiled sweetly. The Pearl *had* sent the car around to pick him and Lulu up. Ruby, Mr Poppet and quite a few other neighbours had piled into the car too. Nobody had been in a stretch limo before.

Crowded around the limo were hordes of people, eager to catch sight of the boy from the newspaper article. There was an enormous 'Oooh!' of delight when they saw his chair. It gleamed so brightly in the sunshine that Lulu had to put her sunglasses on to shield the glare. The crowd had seen nothing like it before.

'I see you've brought your friends,' sneered the Pearl as the endless stream of neighbours piled out of the limo. She caught sight of Ruby's hair and the two little mice running about. She shuddered.

'Mice... at an occasion like this... *really!*' she muttered under her breath to the Meddling Sniveller, who was standing, as usual, by her side. She snapped her fingers and a grovelling assistant squeezed the perfume atomiser in front of her nose.

'Your Pearliness, Hoity-Toitys, La-Di-Das,' announced the Meddling Sniveller through a cordless microphone. 'Oh... I *nearly* forgot... *ladies and gentlemen*. It is with great pleasure that I declare this fairground open. Cameron McPherson, would you do us the honour and cut the ribbon?'

Cameron looked around for reassurance before wheeling his way toward the ribbon. Lulu and Ruby smiled and Mr Poppet winked at him knowingly. Some mates from his school gave him the thumbs up.

The entrance to the fairground was a large, ornate wooden arch with two oriental towers on either side, painted white and silver and decorated with bright, colourful electrical bulbs which flashed off and on. Below the arch was a painted sign which read:

'CAMERON TIBERIUS McPHERSON – HERO OF PIMPLE.'

Cameron's heart filled with pride. *That's my name up there... that's me*, he thought to himself. As he approached the ribbon, everyone in the crowd went quiet.

'Scissors?' whispered Cameron.

'Scissors?' echoed the Pearl, looking around for assistance.

'Scissors? What do you want scissors for, boy?' enquired the Meddling Sniveller impatiently. He bent forward towards Cameron, holding his silver binoculars in one hand to get a better look at him.

'To cut the ribbon of course,' explained Cameron matter-of-factly.

'Blimey, they can't even get this right,' said Lulu to Ruby.

The Pearl clicked her fingers.

'Bag, my bag!' she snarled. An assistant ran forward clutching a large quilted bag and opened it for her. The Pearl rummaged around, muttering to herself, until she discovered what she was looking for.

'Scissors from my last plastic surgery operation,' rejoiced the Pearl. 'My surgeon, Dr Griselda Bundage, gave them to me as a memento.' She brandished them in the air triumphantly before handing them to Cameron.

Cameron took the scissors and had a good look at the Pearl's face, wondering which bits of it were real. Her only distinguishable features were her perfect tombstone teeth. Cameron guessed that these too were probably false. Other than them, she had no real features to speak of. Only two stretched and slanting eyes, a bump with two holes she called a nose and larger-than-life cartoon lips. She looked like a newt.

The red ribbon stretched from one side of the entrance to the other, just waiting to be cut. He took the scissors, slipped his thumb and fingers through the handles and snapped the blades open.

SNIP… SNIP… SNIP.

'These scissors don't work!' said Cameron, handing them back to the Pearl.

No wonder she looks like she does, thought Lulu.

'Impossible! They've worked for me every time!' retorted The Pearl. 'Sniveller, sort it!'

This is taking too long, thought Cameron, reversing his chair.

'Let's get this party started!' he yelled at the top of his voice. Speeding forward, he burst through the ribbon, through the entrance and into the fairground.

The excited crowd swept behind him. The fair was open!

While Cameron waited for his mum and friends to catch up, he was suddenly surrounded by people coming to congratulate him.

'Congratulations, my dear boy. Jolly good effort!'

'Yes, well done, my lad.'

'Good on you, Cam!'

Everyone was in such a good mood and no wonder! The fair was a feast for the senses. The sound of fairground machines whirled overhead; bright lights flashed; neon pink candyfloss spun around sticks; kids licked sticky fingers; there was laughter everywhere.

'All here?' said Lulu, looking around.

'I haven't been to a fair in years!' exclaimed Ruby, patting her hair.

'Even the mice have their own Ferris wheel!' said Mr Poppet, pointing to the mouse wheel in Ruby's hair in which Inky and Poe went round and round.

They were just about to make a move when Cameron's nose twitched. He could smell strawberries and cream, bubblegum, caramel sundaes and banana split. He'd smelled this before. But where? And where was it coming from now? He looked around, past the candyfloss stall and saw a queue of people waiting in front of a pink and sky-blue Volkswagen ice cream van.

Strange, thought Cameron. The van looked familiar but somehow different. On the side of the van was a sliding window but nobody seemed to be inside. From where he was sitting he could just about glimpse a silver spiral staircase in the back of the van, leading to an upper deck that was surrounded by battlements, embossed with ice cream cones holding suns, moons and stars.

'Let's have an ice cream,' said Lulu.

'Just a minute,' said Cameron. He moved his chair to get a better view. And then he saw the sign, emblazoned in colourful letters underneath the window of the van.

'MR PEA'S DREAMY ICE CREAM.'

'Wow! It's Mr Pea... *Mr Pea!* He's here selling ice creams... but where is he?' Cameron wheeled over to the front of the queue to see him. The others followed closely. Lulu was eager to reunite with the man who had saved her life.

At that very moment, Mr Pea popped his head out of the van's side window.

'Hello, little fella. Thought I'd surprise you!' He laughed out loud, leaned further out of the window and shook Cameron's hand. 'And your sweet mama's here too!'

'So glad to see you again, Mr Pea, under more favourable conditions,' replied Lulu.

'You're back!' exclaimed Cameron. He couldn't

quite believe it. He was so thrilled to see Mr Pea again.

'I thought you and your friends would like to try some of my dreamy-tasting ice cream,' said Mr Pea, gesturing to the ever-growing queue of people.

Cameron nodded enthusiastically but he was a little puzzled. 'The van... it looks different.'

'My little van can be whatever you want it to be,' said Mr Pea. 'Remember what you thought you saw, the day of the tornado!' And with that, he tapped his fingers on the laminated worktop and started to rap.

'All your favourite flavours, floating round your brain,
Mixed all up fantastically. No two will taste the same,
My magic wafer cones are full of cosmic flavour,
Delicious tasting dreams – to slurp, to lick, to savour.'

'Now what flavour would the guest of honour like?' asked Mr Pea.

Cameron thought of all his favourite flavours. 'Chocolate chip, strawberries, caramel and banana split, please!'

'One Cameron Special coming up!' said Mr Pea. He grabbed his ice cream scoop and placed a big dollop of cream-coloured ice cream onto a wafer cone.

'It looks just like vanilla,' said Cameron, a little disappointed.

'Ah! That's where the *magic* comes in. Taste it and see.'

Cameron licked and slurped the ice cream cone.

'Oooh! Wow! Yummy! This is the most delicious ice cream I've ever tasted. It tastes of… everything I thought of!'

With that, the queue of people all started to push to the front, shouting out their favourite flavours. Lulu had crushed blackberry, hazelnut and cherry. Ruby picked lavender and rose-water, and Mr Poppet chose only one flavour – coffee, *strong* coffee.

Cameron, Lulu, Ruby and Mr Poppet licked their lips clean until every last trace of delicious, sticky, dreamy ice cream was gone.

'Let's go on some rides,' said Cameron, when he was absolutely, positively, 100 percent sure not a drop was left.

'Good idea, little fella. I'll see ya all later!' chuckled Mr Pea, serving fox and pheasant ice cream to a particularly large Hoity-Toity.

The Ferris wheel was huge! 'WHEEE!' squealed Cameron, as he rocked the passenger carriage at the top. The ground seemed a very long way down. He could see Mr Poppet in the carriage below, squeezed in next to Ruby and her wide crinoline, and he chatted noisily with his mum above the fairground hum, waiting for the remaining carriages on the ground to be filled. Everyone wanted a ride. Eventually the Ferris wheel started to turn. The flashing spokes changed colour to the beat of the music. Down below, he could see little children bobbing up and down on the nearby carousel. Little hands waved from colourfully painted horses, a merry-go-round of laughter. It was all such fun.

Cameron's second ride was on a rollercoaster called 'the Star Screamer'.

'I'm not sure about this one,' said Lulu as she climbed into the first coaster car next to Cameron. The safety bar slammed down. *CLUNK!*

The coaster car rattled its way slowly up the steep track of the enormous metal loop-di-loop.

Cameron laughed nervously as the car stopped for a full ten seconds at the top of the rollercoaster. They held their breaths in anticipation. It was a long way down.

'Aaaagghh!' they screamed, as the coaster car rattled down the steep metal curve of the rollercoaster at terrifying speed.

'No hands!' shouted Cameron, throwing his arms up in the air.

'Noooo! I can't look,' shouted Lulu, closing her eyes. It was terrifying and exhilarating all at the same time. The car sped along. They couldn't stop laughing!

*

Cameron was having a blast. He'd never had so much fun. A day of rides and fairground fun, bumper cars and rotating twister machines, magical ice cream and candy floss. What could be better?

'I don't know about anybody else,' said Lulu cheerily, 'but I'd like to go to the karaoke tent. I think I feel an Elvis song coming on. Anyone up for it?'

Cameron looked at Mr Poppet and Mr Poppet looked at Ruby. Nobody looked at Lulu. Mr Poppet muttered he needed the toilet and quickly Cameron said he did too – which left Lulu staring at Ruby.

Ruby recalled she had some earplugs – essential for parachuting on windy days. She could always pop them in and cover her ears with her cascading white curls. Lulu would never notice.

'I'd be *delighted* to accompany you,' said Ruby.

'Have fun, boys!' called Lulu as she belted towards the karaoke tent. Ruby followed behind, stuffing the plugs into her ears in preparation.

'Err... Umm... I don't really need to go to the toilet,' confessed Cameron.

'Try what?' asked Mr Poppet, mishearing.

'The toilet! I don't really need to go.'

'Me neither!' said Mr Poppet, giving him a wink.

'What are we going to do then?' asked Cameron.

'Let's visit some of the stalls,' proposed Mr Poppet. 'There's still a lot to see.' He'd had enough of fairground rides. He wanted to stretch his legs.

So they wandered off through the fair. They threw wooden balls at the coconut shy, tried tossing hoops over large pastel-coloured stuffed toys (no luck) until, at the edge of the fairground, an orange tent caught Cameron's eye. It was decorated with gold foil cutouts of sphinxes, just like the ones on his wheelchair. A sign hung, reading: 'FORTUNE TELLING – LET THE SPHINXES REVEAL YOUR FUTURE!'

'*Sphinxes* again.' Cameron remembered what Ruby had told him. Sphinxes represented truth and secrets, mysteries and riddles. His mum had often had her fortune told, usually coming back with predictions of how she would soon marry again and get an even longer surname.

'This looks good. I wouldn't mind a go,' volunteered Mr Poppet.

'Let's go for it,' said Cameron. They approached the fortune telling tent. A tall man stood outside wearing a long hessian robe. He looked like a monk. His face was hidden inside a deep hood and a long beard dangled from his pointy chin.

'Come inside,' said the man, beckoning with his long finger. 'Let the sphinxes speak through the mystery of the crystal ball.' Cameron was intrigued.

Sphinxes, mysteries and crystal balls. He was definitely up for some fortune telling.

The hooded man turned around just as Mr Poppet was about to enter.

'Only one at a time, mister,' he growled, wagging his finger in front of Mr Poppet. 'I can't concentrate if there are too many people in the space. Come back in ten minutes.'

What an extraordinarily long finger! thought Mr Poppet. 'I'll grab myself a doughnut and hook me-a-duck while I'm waiting,' he decided, wandering off.

The tent was dark apart from a few flickering candles which threw strange shadows against the canvas. Cameron sat in his chair opposite the fortune teller. A small table stood in between them with a crystal ball placed in the middle. The crystal ball was as big as his goldfish bowl at home and stood on a wooden base carved with dragons. It was made from opaque glass and different colours pulsated from the centre.

The hooded man grabbed Cameron's right hand, turning it upwards to look at his palm.

'Your life has been *transformed* in the last few days,' the mysterious man said. 'Nothing will ever be the same. I'll reveal some more of your incredible future soon for you are a very *special* boy.'

Cameron was hooked. *Incredible future, eh? I*

wonder what else he's going to tell me. But just then he noticed the shape of another hooded figure, standing perfectly still, set back behind the fortune teller.

'Who's he?' asked Cameron nervously.

'He's my medium. I need to channel my energy through him in order to speak to spirits on the other side,' insisted the fortune teller. 'Don't you worry about a thing,' he added reassuringly. 'Just *look* into the crystal ball. *Look* into the crystal ball.'

Cameron stared intently into the colourful light. It first pulsated a deep red colour, then faded to pink, glowed to yellow, then faded to green. Blue to purple... Orange to violet... With every pulse of light, every change of colour, Cameron's eyelids got heavier and heavier. The fortune teller's buttery tones washed over Cameron as he repeated and repeated, '*Look* into the crystal ball. *Look* into the crystal ball.' Within minutes Cameron was mesmerised, unaware of everything and everyone around him. Spellbound by the hypnotic, pulsing light. His heavy eyelids closed and he fell into a deep, deep sleep.

Little did he know he had been hypnotised. Hypnotised by the devious and slippery Erikson Longfingers!

'We 'ave to act quickly!' whispered the other man as he pulled off his hood to reveal Monsieur Cornichon. Both men snapped into action, quickly lifting Cameron out of his chair and laying him on the ground.

'We've only got an hour before he comes round,' said Longfingers. He took a large blanket from underneath the table and used it to cover Cameron's wheelchair. It was so recognisable, it could give the whole game away.

'Come on, come on!' screeched Cornichon. He opened up a leather hold-all bag and took out a bundle of clothing. They took off their hooded gowns and quickly got changed.

When they'd finished dressing, they looked quite different. Cornichon was now disguised as an old lady with purple stockings, an ill-fitting worsted wool suit and a moth-eaten fox fur wrapped around his neck. Perched on his head was a matted grey wig with a wide brimmed hat with a felt trim and a pheasant feather sticking out at a jaunty angle. Longfingers was more soberly attired, in a smart brown suit and a trilby hat. He checked that his false beard was secure.

'Right, let's go!'

'If anyone asks who I am, remember I am your grandmozzer!' said Cornichon, adjusting his wig and putting on some steel framed glasses. He spoke in a high-pitched female voice and affected a stooping posture in order to appear old and frail.

'You look hideous,' said Longfingers.

'This is no time for joking, you fool!' snapped Cornichon, getting into the chair.

Longfingers bent down to check the sleeping figure of Cameron on the floor.

'This one's out for the count,' he sniggered. 'Good! We'll be well on our way by the time he wakes up.'

He pushed the chair with Cornichon sitting in it, through the back entrance of the tent into the daylight, into the hustle and bustle of the crowds. As they entered the busy fairgrounds and mingled, the crowds were oblivious to the dastardly criminals in their midst. They were simply a normal man in a brown suit and his invalid grandmother.

Mr Poppet was just about to have a shot on the rifle range when he spotted Lulu and Ruby walking towards him.

'Where's Cameron?' asked Lulu.

'He's having his fortune told.' Mr Poppet chuckled. 'The tent's just over there.' He pointed to the 'FORTUNE TELLING' sign. 'A tall chap's doing it... a bearded chap... longest fingers I've ever seen in my life!'

Lulu's heart missed a beat. Could it be? Surely not! That dreadful Longfingers didn't have a beard. But then she remembered his fingers around her neck that terrible night in the lake – his long, powerful fingers… She ran towards the tent as fast as she could and burst in.

It was dark inside after the bright light of the day. She could smell smoke from newly extinguished candles and her eyes were drawn to the crystal ball glowing in the centre of the tent. But where was Cameron? Panic took over. As her eyes adjusted to the dim light, she could make out a figure lying on the floor. It was her boy! Dear oh dear! Was he alive? What was he doing on the floor? Where was his chair?

'Cameron, my love, speak to me!' she sobbed as she knelt down beside him. She put her ear to his heart. He was breathing. She kissed his cheek and felt his warm breath. She gently stroked his hair, his hands, lovingly whispering, 'Cameron, *Cameron!*'

— CHAPTER TWENTY —

JUST DESSERTS

Cameron opened his eyes. 'Mum, where am I?'
'Thank goodness... *thank goodness!*' cried Lulu.
Ruby and Mr Poppet dashed in. Mr Poppet was horrified to see Cameron lying on the floor.

'Oh dear, what happened? I'm *so* sorry. I should have stayed with him!'

'Now's not the time,' interrupted Lulu. 'Just go and get the police! Cameron's OK, I think, but somebody has stolen his chair.'

Mr Poppet ran as fast as his legs could carry him. Ruby bobbed along next to him, her wide crinoline dress crashing into the oncoming crowds of people.

'Help! Help! Police!'

Ruby soon ran into the policeman she had met in the park and despite his initial hesitation – *not this mad woman again!* – he quickly called for backup. Within minutes, two police cars had arrived. Blue lights flashed and the sounds of sirens filled the air.

Longfingers and Cornichon were very near the exit when they heard the sounds of the sirens.

'Push 'arder for goodness' sake!' yelled Cornichon. He could see the white and silver towers of the entrance.

'Almost there, Granny!' puffed Longfingers. It wasn't easy pushing Cornichon around in Cameron's chair. At first, the chair had seemed unbelievably easy to push but it had gradually become heavy and cumbersome. If he pushed it in one direction, it veered in another. It was as if it had a mind of its own.

As Cornichon and Longfingers turned the corner, the metallic screech of trumpets blasted in their ears. A uniformed brass band marched straight toward them and cut across their pathway to freedom.

'Aaaagh!' shrieked Cornichon, rubbing his cheek where the slide from an advancing trombone had struck his face.

Longfingers pushed the wheelchair this way and that, weaving in and out of the marching musicians. The trumpets roared, the trombones ripped and the tubas rumbled.

'DO something!' screamed Cornichon. The noise from the brass band was deafening. Longfingers was trying to make his way through a small gap between the percussion and the flugelhorn when he got another surprise. Troupes of dancing majorettes, twirling their batons in the air, were coming towards them.

'For 'eaven sake, we 'ave to get out of 'ere!' hissed
Cornichon, ducking his head to avoid the rhythmic
high kick from a rather enthusiastic majorette.

'Blast!' cursed Longfingers, turning around. The
only escape route he could see was across some open
ground. There was a problem though. In order to do
this, he had to pass the Hoity-Toitys and the La-Di-
Das. The two opposing groups of the Assembly were
having a private party. Sectioned off from the rest of
the fairground with purple- and green-twined rope,
they were being served canapés and champagne, all
under the watchful eye of Paloma Snuck.

Longfingers and Cornichon tried to be as
invisible as possible as they attempted to sneak past.
Unfortunately, the blanket covering the golden
wheelchair caught underneath the wheel and started
to pull itself off the chair. Cornichon quickly lent
over the side and tried to pull the blanket back up.
The wig slipped off his sweaty head. As he tried to
re-adjust it, he caught the eye of Paloma Snuck.

'*Monsieur Cornichon!*' blurted Paloma. She was so
shocked at seeing her old employer again that she
dropped her tray of pig's trotters and fisheye
canapés. The Hoity-Toitys and the La-Di-Das all
turned as one at the mention of Cornichon's name.
The traitor was in their midst! Paloma then noticed
the man pushing Cornichon. She knew that profile!

'*Mr Longfingers!*'

'Ze stupid girl 'as recognised us. Quick, back into ze crowd!' shrieked Cornichon.

Longfingers didn't know which way to go. To the left or to the right? To the left was the hustle and the bustle of the fairground... but also flashing blue police lights. To the right was open ground... but also a mob of Hoity-Toitys and La-Di-Das who had spilled out from beyond the purple and green rope and were angrily approaching.

Longfingers quickly made a decision. He certainly didn't want to be lynched by the Hoity-Toitys and the La-Di-Das. He pushed the chair back into the bustling crowd.

As they entered the throng, they noticed two policemen heading in their direction.

'Do something and make it *quick!*' insisted Cornichon.

Longfingers thought this would be as good a time as any to find out if the chair really did fly. There weren't, after all, that many options left. He needed the chair to transform. Now!

'Fly, for goodness' sake, *fly!*' he pleaded, thinking of the little brat's flying machine.

The chair started to vibrate gently... *brr*... then violently... *BRR... BRR... BRR!* It shook and rattled like a washing machine on a full spin cycle. And then it rotated, slowly at first, increasing momentum as it spun around.

'Noooooo!' screamed Longfingers.

Longfingers' feet left the ground. He tried to release his hands but found they were stuck to the chair's handles.

'What the blazes?' he exclaimed loudly.

'I can't move out of ze *chaaaaair!*' shrieked Cornichon, finding he too was stuck to the seat.

ZZZZ... ZZZZ... ZZZZ went the chair as it whizzed around faster and faster.

'Oooh! Aaah!' cried the crowd.

WHIZZ... BUZZ... the chair rose into the air, twirling around like an orbital fairground ride, out of control. The gold metal caught the sun and reflected a blinding golden light. *HUM... THRUM...* it spun and spun, shook and rattled high above the ground. You could just about hear Erickson Longfingers and Monsieur Cornichon's screams.

Lulu was pushing Cameron through the crowds in a small collapsible wheelchair which the police had brought from the first-aid tent. He wanted to get closer to the action. He *wanted* to find his magical wheelchair!

Then, looking up, he saw the golden, spinning chair light up in the air.

'That's *my chair!*' he shouted at the top of his voice. And as soon as he uttered the words, it happened.

'Ooooh!' boomed the crowd dramatically. The chair had stopped spinning and was now hovering, suspended, utterly still...

For a split second.

WHOOSH! The chair and its passengers started to fall... *CRASH!* Right to the ground with a mighty thump!

The crowd fell silent. For a moment, Cornichon and Longfingers didn't move. Stars flashed in front of their eyes. They groaned as they came to. Longfingers' hat and beard had come off and he was covered in bruises. Cornichon's grey wig had also fallen off, revealing his sweaty bald head.

The crowd started to laugh as they both tried to crawl towards the flashing bulbs that marked the entrance, in a last ditch attempt to escape.

Cornichon staggered and swayed as he picked himself up from the ground. He ran with as much speed as he could muster towards the nearby crowd. *TWANG* went the elastic on his purple stockings. They slid down his thighs, over his knobbly knees and gathered around his ankles. Cornichon toddled along precariously for a second until... *SPLAT!* He fell, face first, into the mud.

'You're coming with us, dear!' announced a policeman, grabbing Cornichon by the arm and escorting him to the police car.

While everyone was concentrating on Cornichon,

Longfingers saw his window of opportunity and made a run for it. He *had* to make it to the open ground. He burst through the gathered Hoity-Toitys and La-Di-Das in a last desperate attempt for freedom. Champagne glasses went flying, canapés dropped into the mud.

'Out of my way!'

Paloma Snuck wasn't having any of it. She stuck her foot out, just as Longfingers barged past. Longfingers tripped and lurched forward – straight into the La-Di-Da's commemorative trifle! His head sunk into the jellied mackerel and catfish custard. He was beaten. Beaten by Paloma Snuck.

'Not such a smarty pants now, are we?' chuckled a policeman, handcuffing a slimy-trifled Longfingers and marching him to the waiting police car.

The crowd followed the police car out as it left the fairground. Word had spread that these two men were the jewel thieves. Pimple had never had so much drama!

'Be nice to each other, boys, you'll be spending a long time in jail together!' teased the policeman as the two scoundrels bickered in the back of the carover who was to blame for their capture. The blue light spun around on top of the police car and the siren wailed once more as Longfingers and Cornichon sped off towards their new dank, cold, undecorated home.

The wheelchair stood where it had fallen,

perfectly erect, without a scratch or dent or blemish. Lulu brushed the seat with her hand, sweeping away the pheasant's feather from Cornichon's hat. It was the only remnant left from that dastardly duo. She picked Cameron up from the collapsible wheelchair and placed him back in his chair.

'I bet that chair could tell a few stories,' remarked Mr Poppet.

'*I* could tell a few stories!' Cameron laughed. It felt good to be sitting in his wheelchair again. His *chariot*.

'Well, my dears, I'm off,' Ruby announced. 'I've had quite enough excitement for one day. Besides, it's Inky and Poe's supper time. *Au revoir, mon chéris, au revoir!*' And with a wave of her hand, Ruby headed for home, her crinoline bobbing merrily into the distance.

'I'm going to join her. Toodle-oo, everyone!' said Mr Poppet.

'We ought to think about making a move too,' said Lulu. 'It's been another long day.'

'I wonder if Mr Pea would take us home?' said Cameron. 'It would be nice to go home in the Dream Factory Van.'

Cameron and Lulu walked over to the van and found Mr Pea clearing up.

'Hey, little fella. How's tings? Did you have an exciting day?'

'Oh, Mr Pea, the baddies hypnotised me and stole my chair, and I went on fantastic rides, and I had the best ice cream on the planet!' gushed Cameron.

'Well I *never!* The adventures of Cameron and his chair continue,' Mr Pea said with a laugh.

'They *certainly* do,' said Lulu. She cast her mind back over the past few days: parachuting neighbours, jewel-stealing criminals, food fights, magical wheelchairs, nearly drowning… Right now, she just wanted to sit on her sofa with her legs up, sipping a nice cup of tea.

'Time to go home. I'll drop you off,' said Mr Pea, looking at Lulu.

'You read my mind. But can we go the more conventional route?'

'Through the town?' said Mr Pea.

'Through the town,' repeated Lulu and Cameron at the same time. After the extraordinary week they'd both had, an ordinary drive through their ordinary town sounded like a good idea.

They were all sitting in the front seat of the Dream Factory Van when the Pearl of Pimple and the Meddling Sniveller stuck their heads through the window.

'You and your chair saved the day… Pimple's little hero,' grovelled the Sniveller.

'The Limousine awaits you dear, *dear* Cameron,' gushed the Pearl.

'No, thank you,' said Cameron firmly. 'We're going home in the Intergalactic Dream Factory Van.'

'An *ice cream van!* Instead of a stretch limousine! Well, *really!*' said the Pearl. She and the Meddling Sniveller pulled their heads back from the window like retreating tortoises, and the Pearl stuck her nose up and pompously sniffed the air. Unfortunately, at that very moment, her attendant squeezed the perfume atomiser in front of her, causing her to cough and splutter.

'See you later, alligator,' Lulu said with a laugh.

'In a while, crocodile!' Cameron chuckled, remembering how the Pearl had looked during the food fight.

And with that, they drove home. Past the tall Post Office Tower and the brand new shopping mall, through Pimple High Street and past the iron gates of Gitwick Gardens, past the police station and the Assembly buildings.

Cameron popped his head out of the window. Dark clouds were building in the sky and he could hear the rumble of thunder. Another storm was brewing. The rain started to pitter-patter on the roof, quickly building to a cacophony as the heavens opened.

Mr Pea looked up and smiled to himself. A storm had brought him to Pimple and now a storm would take him away. He had other places to visit.

By the time the Intergalactic Dream Factory Van arrived back at Grimthorpe Towers, the heavy rain had passed though thunder continued to rumble in the distance. Mr Pea drove through the last few puddles before parking the van in the forecourt.

He hopped out and walked around to the passenger seat. Cameron was sitting in his golden wheelchair next to Lulu. There was plenty of room in the magical van.

'I can't say goodbye without a *little* bit of magic now, can I?' said Mr Pea pointedly to Lulu. He waved his hand. There was a flash of light and a silver star-dusted ramp appeared, shimmering in the early evening sun.

Mr Pea beckoned Cameron toward him with his hand. The golden wheelchair moved forward and glided down the magical ramp.

'Talk about tripping the light fantastic!' enthused Lulu as she floated down the stardust slope, swaying her hands from side to side like a dancer in an old Hollywood film.

Mr Pea clicked his fingers and the silver ramp disappeared, leaving only a trail of silver dust. He looked up at the sky to see a new rainbow.

'It's time,' said Mr Pea, looking at Cameron.

'Will I ever see you again, Mr Pea?' asked Cameron.

Mr Pea crouched down and ruffled Cameron's

hair with his hand. The silver beads in his long dreadlocks jangled.

'I've got other places to visit, other people to help, little fella. But I'll always be in *there*, guiding you.' He tapped Cameron's forehead with his finger. 'Havin' a magical chair is a *big* responsibility, my friend. But just be careful what you wish for.'

'Goodbye, Mr Pea, and thank you,' said Lulu, leaning up to kiss him on the cheek.

'High five, Mr Pea,' said Cameron, trying to put on a brave face.

'High five, little fella,' said Mr Pea, slapping Cameron's hand.

Mr Pea jumped into the front of the Intergalactic Dream Factory Van and started the engine. The round headlights flashed orange and purple. The twisted exhaust pipe blew out thick purple smoke and the air filled again with the smell of toffee and pineapple. He waved goodbye as he drove the van to the large puddle at the end of the forecourt. A puddle at the end of a rainbow. Mr Pea drove quickly through it, sending splashes of red, orange, yellow, green, blue, indigo and violet spattering on the ground as the Intergalactic Dream Factory Van left the ground and drove up the rainbow highway.

Cameron watched as the pink and sky-blue van,

with its light-green trim, got smaller and smaller, until it became nothing but a speck in the dusky summer sky.

'Let's put the kettle on,' said Lulu. 'I'm gasping for cuppa!'

'Me too,' said Cameron quietly. He rubbed his eyes with his hand. He didn't want his mum to see.

Later that evening, lying in his bed, Cameron thought about the events of this extraordinary summer holiday. Next week he'd be back at school and things would be different. He would have to choose the right time to use his magical chair from now on.

But as he lay there, listening to the gentle murmur coming from the telly in the living room, he realised this was just the beginning. The beginning of a lifetime full of exciting adventures.

Sure, he wouldn't be able to conquer Gaul like Julius Caesar but he could work on conquering his fears. And OK, he wouldn't be able to march across the mountains like Hannibal but with the help of his chair, he'd be able to walk and dance, maybe even run. So what if he wouldn't be able to conquer the high seas like Horatio Nelson? He'd already retrieved stolen treasure from the bottom of a lake and he was pretty sure the great admiral had never managed that one!

He'd proven to himself that he was brave, that

he had courage and strength and that he could overcome all obstacles in his way.

He snuggled his head into his pillow, heard the click of a switch and watched as an envelope of light slipped under the door from the hallway lamp. His eyelids got heavier and heavier as he thought about maybe, one day, being an astronaut, exploring space and reaching his hand out to touch the stars.